Deadly Desserts

A Small Town Culinary Cozy Mystery

The Cozy Café Mysteries
Book 5

C. A. Phipps

Dedication

For my husband, who makes my life better every day.

Cheryl

Deadly Desserts

A plea from the past cannot be ignored!

While her sisters fought hard to keep the cafe alive, Ruby Finch had her eye on becoming the town librarian. It took a death for that to come about which wasn't ideal.

Now she's helping her fiancé with his new diner, the site of a murder and then arson, and wondering why bad things keep happening.

When she finds a note with a plea for help, Ruby can't agree with the sheriff that it is a hoax or a joke. Thankfully her sisters trust her intuition. The three of them dig deep into a rich family's history knowing it isn't welcome.

Knowing it could be very dangerous.

The Cozy Café mysteries are light, cozy mysteries featuring a family-focused café owner, a librarian, and an antiques dealer who discover they are talented amateur sleuths—and magnets for animals.

Other books in the series:
Book 1 Sweet Saboteur
Book 2 Candy Corruption
Book 3 Mocha Mayhem
Book 4 Berry Betrayal
Book 5 Deadly Desserts

Enjoy a FREE recipe or two in every book!

Join my new release mailing list and pick up a free recipe book!

Chapter One

Ruby smiled wistfully as she stood at the library window sharing the view of Main Street with George, the Finch family's large tabby cat. The hustle and bustle in and around the Cozy Café up the street tugged at her heart—some days more than others. As much as she loved her job as the town's librarian, she missed baking with her two sisters in the café their mother had owned. Now that the three of them had their lives more or less sorted, that naturally meant spending less time together.

Perhaps sensing her nostalgia, a wet nose nudged her hand and she absently scratched Bob the chocolate Labrador's ears. The dog had been asleep under her desk and now he whined. She crouched to hug him. "What's the matter boy?"

"He knows I am here." A big hand touched her shoulder, accompanying the gruff voice. Gruff, yet also filled with concern. "Are you okay?"

"Sheesh!" Ruby stood clutching her throat. A giant of a man, Alexander moved with the grace of a cat. "You scared me half to death, but yeah I'm fine. Just being silly. I miss my sisters."

His blue eyes blinked in astonishment. "I am sorry that I frightened you, I did not sneak, but you were deep in thought. Tell me how it is possible to miss Scarlett and Violet when you live in the same house and see them every day?"

"See?" She raised both hands. "Feeling blue about it is ridiculous."

"You could never be ridiculous," the big Russian said, clearly upset that she would take his words to heart.

She patted one of his bulging biceps. "Thank you. My weird mood is obviously due to all the recent changes in our lives. While we do live in the same house, it feels like we're drifting apart. I don't like it."

Alex gently lifted her chin with a finger. "Then you must prevent it from getting worse," he told her matter-of-factly, as if this were the easiest thing in the world to do. "Or reverse it."

"Reverse it? How can I do that?"

His brows knitted and then he smiled. "You like to bake together. Why not spend an hour every morning at your mother's bakery making your favorite cakes before you open the library and Violet's antique store?"

She gasped at the simplicity of it. "And that answer is one more reason why I love you."

He kissed her nose. "Tell me more of these reasons."

Though she loved his attention, Ruby placed a palm against his shirt, feeling the hard lines of his chest beneath. "Oh no you don't. I have work to do and your diner is due to open in a few days. I'm pretty sure you have plenty to keep you occupied as well."

He gave a slight bow. "You are right as always. I have

been ticking off the list you made for all the little things you say I must organize."

"Trust me, you'll be glad when you open and everything is at your fingertips. You're going to be so busy that if you don't do it now, you'll be at sixes and sevens."

He frowned so hard that she almost laughed. He didn't always understand her Americanisms and it frustrated him. Born near the Ukraine border, Alex desperately wanted to be considered one of them and she wanted him to believe he was. No one could look at Alexander and think he had confidence issues, but they were there alright.

"It means that you will be in a mess," she explained.

"I do not wish that," he said fervently.

"No you don't, my love." She tapped his nose. "Not if you want repeat customers."

The frown did not leave and she stood on tiptoe to smooth his forehead with her fingertips. "Are you still worried about the menu?"

He nodded sadly. "I want the people in Cozy Hollow to like my food."

"They will. I promise."

The look on his face was a mixture of doubt and hope. He wanted to believe her, but having had many promises broken in the past, mainly from his father, he was wary of them. "How can you know this for sure?"

"Because me and my sisters know food, and we say so. Everything you make is delicious. Honestly, the fusion of Russian and American cuisine is a winner," she gushed, knowing it was the truth.

He considered this and his eventual smile lit the slightly dim library like no light ever could.

"Like you and me?"

"Exactly." Happy now that they were both reassured,

Ruby kissed his cheek before walking him to the front door. "Thanks again for picking up those boxes from Gail Norman yesterday afternoon."

He shrugged and flexed his muscles. "It was nothing. I hope you have a good day and I will have lunch ready for you at 12 o'clock."

Ruby tried not to plead. "Just a salad will be fine."

He shook his head firmly. "I think not. I need to practice as much as I can."

"So, I'm your guinea pig again?" she teased.

He grimaced. "You are a flower, not some pig."

A snort escaped her. He'd get the hang of the language a lot better now that he wasn't hiding away in a woodcutter's hut as he had done since his father, a rich businessman, brought him into the country several years ago. Now that everyone knew his parentage there were no secrets and Alex could be whoever he wanted to be. Which just happened to be a chef in his own diner.

He kissed her goodbye and Ruby's toes curled. She could never imagine getting tired of her giant and his unique personality. He was so focused and determined and yet in his mind he wasn't convinced he was good enough. Her mission was to make him see that he was better than good. He was talented and truly cared about people.

She sighed as she watched him stroll down the street, his movements fluid and graceful. The large black dog who had been waiting outside, and was disdainful of being inside anywhere, nudged Alex's hand until it rested on the football sized head. They were a good pair. Crossing the road they disappeared around the back of the diner.

Ruby shook herself back to reality and returned to her desk and the boxes waiting there. Using one of the old cloths she kept for this purpose, she wiped the top of the first one. Though covered in dust, inside were treasures and she opened it with excitement building.

George came to sit on the desk, looking decidedly annoyed that he had such little space.

"Stop glaring at me. You have the whole library to stretch out in, including two couches. The boxes will be gone by tomorrow and then you can have your spot back. Although, you might want to consider that it is also my spot."

He gave her a disdainful glance and made his way back to a patch of sunshine coming in the front window. Bob stayed with her and curled around a desk leg. It seemed like she spent half her day trying not to trip over the big goofball, but somehow she didn't mind at all.

She grinned and reached into the box. The first book was an early edition of Jane Austen and the others on this layer looked to be of the same era. Her heart fluttered. Not in the way Alex made it flutter, but this was another kind of love. Books made her heart sing. As many as she could get her hands on would never be enough and putting them into the hands of other people who loved them too was a passion that would never wane.

Ruby did have a huge issue. A part of her wanted to personally keep special books like this. Unfortunately, it warred with her desire to have them available to all customers. However a book from the 1800's wouldn't be suitable for lending to multiple people at a library.

She held the book reverently and opened it carefully, prepared to worry about the logistics later. It was so well kept, despite the appearance of the boxes, and she felt sure the others would be in just as good a condition. Flicking the pages slowly, she smiled at the smell and old-fashioned typeset.

A piece of paper slipped to the floor.

She replaced the book and bent to pick it up. Her eyes widening as the first words stood out from all the rest.

Help me.

I am an unworthy embarrassment to the family.

Someone to be hidden away.

I just want to be free.

Ruby's breath came quickly as she turned the note over in her hand. There was no signature and nothing else. Who wrote it? And, more importantly, when?

Chapter Two

The front door opened and the sudden breeze made the note flutter in Ruby's hand.

"Hey, Rubes. I saw Alex leave and thought I'd pop over before anyone else arrives and check if you opened ..." Violet Finch stopped as she reached the desk and frowned. "What's wrong?"

It was annoying that she wore her feelings so openly, but Ruby was glad to see her middle sister. "I just found this." She handed Violet the note.

"Wow! That's intense. Where was it?"

"In this book." Ruby pulled it back out of the box and gave it to her sister.

"Can I assume that these are the books from the Swanson estate?"

Ruby waved her hand at the four boxes on the desk. "They all are."

"To think that I only stopped by to see if there were any suitable books you would part with for my store." Violet snorted. "I wasn't expecting a mystery."

There was a moment's silence as they swapped a look of

disbelief. Since their mom's death they had been embroiled in one mystery after another and while it was no longer shocking, it was always a surprise.

"It wasn't on my radar either," Ruby told her.

Violet nodded. "She did mention it but remind me how Gail Norman got these books to donate to the library."

"When her cousin Agatha Swanson passed away, Agatha's son Edgar wanted everything out of the house. He let the family come and choose from things he didn't want. Gail said most of the good stuff was gone by the time she got there and was scared all the remaining books would get dumped. Then she thought of me and the library."

"There must be quite a few in these boxes. Are they all this good?"

"I won't know until I open them. To be honest, when Gail said that they were old, it occurred to me that some might suit your store better than the library. I want to have as wide a range as I can fit in, but people keep giving me their cast-offs." Ruby sighed. "Which is lovely when they're in decent condition and others might be interested, but often they aren't either of those things and the donors are merely getting rid of junk—a word I hate to use in connection with books." She touched the box reverently. "Unlike these beauties."

It made Ruby sad to discard any book no matter the condition. What she couldn't use, if they had some life left in them, she sent to the school in an even smaller town where Alex had lived before he moved here. Harmony Beach was a poor community; despite the wealth of the wood industry it had grown from. That industry was represented in the area by the Carver Corporation—owned by Alex's father, who was not her favorite person due to how he had treated his illegitimate son.

Violet turned the book over in her hand. "Well, if they are all like this, they'll definitely be worth something."

Pushing down the residual anger over thinking of how Alex had been hurt by a man who should have done better, Ruby smiled. "If you help me pull them all out, we can look through them together and speed up the process."

"Quit the over-sweet expression. You are so good at getting people to do stuff for you, but I think you forget that I'm your sister and I know your games."

Ruby sniffed. "I have no idea what you mean."

"Sure you don't," Violet scoffed and proceeded to pull the books out and carefully lay them on a small table Ruby had set up behind the desk for this purpose. "You're in luck I can spare an hour or two now. Gail's in the shop early this morning and I told her I might be a while."

"It's really working out for the two of you sharing the premises. And you're the best," Ruby simpered, earning her a rolling of eyes and she laughed. It never failed to give her a warm buzz that she and Violet had found their passion and were living their dreams in their home town. She considered that a librarian and an antique dealer were also somewhat alike. They both loved to take care of the items in their possession and understood the value of them, which was not always monetary. Although, that did cause a slight conundrum for Ruby.

"If you take and sell some of the books, will you give Gail something?"

Violet nodded. "Definitely. I was thinking 50/50."

Ruby smiled. "I never really doubted it, but it's good to know for sure."

Violet shook her head. "You and Scarlett always have to have everything in black and white."

Scarlett the oldest of the sisters struggled with OCD

and took charge of their mom's bakery when Lilac Finch got sick and then passed away a few years ago.

Ruby shrugged. "It leaves nothing up in the air and causes less confusion that way. And I'm willing to bet that this is exactly how you treat your business when people ask the price of something and then want to beat you down."

"Hmm. I never thought of it like that. I guess you're right."

Ruby shrugged. "I usually am according to Alex."

Violet chuckled. "That man is so wrapped around your finger he'd say anything to make you happy."

"And your point is?" Ruby feigned annoyance.

"That you are one lucky woman."

"Now, that is the truth." Ruby grinned. "Although, to be fair, he is also one lucky man."

Violet rolled her eyes. "If only people heard the real Ruby, they wouldn't have you pinned firmly as the sweet and innocent that you portray."

"And yet you never deny it, except to the family."

"Because we both know it wouldn't do me a lick of good."

They were still laughing when Scarlett came through the door with a covered plate. The smell was heavenly and they raced to her side to see what goodies she had brought them.

"I could hear you two from up the street. "What's got you both in such a good mood?" Scarlett's eyes twinkled. "Oh, wait. I guess it's all these old books."

Violet and Ruby each snatched a blueberry muffin from the plate and bit into the pillow of goodness.

"Mmm. So good," Violet said around a mouthful.

Ruby nodded and handed Scarlett the note so as not to interrupt her enjoyment.

"What the heck?" Scarlett gasped, not bothered about any such interruptions. "Who wrote this?"

Ruby swallowed and sighed. The rest of the muffin would have to wait. Once a Finch sister got a whiff of a mystery the world receded. "We don't know exactly, but it must have been someone in the Swanson household since that's where the book came from."

"That big estate on the way to Harmony Beach?"

"That's it." Violet spoke around a mouthful.

Scarlett wrinkled her nose. "So you think a family member wrote the note?"

"Or staff," Ruby told her. "According to Gail, they were incredibly wealthy once upon a time and it looks like the note was written a while ago."

Scarlett let out a huff of breath. "Oh, that's good. I'd hate to think we had another murder to solve. So, why was Gail given these books if they're worth something?"

"Now that his mother is dead, Mr. Swanson wants to clear the place of everything that isn't his or has some significance to him. He already held an auction, but the books were in the garage and not found until Gail was looking for something to take from the estate. It was a condition of Agatha's will that her remaining cousins got to choose something."

Scarlett tutted. "So he didn't think the books were worth anything?"

Ruby's mouthed pursed. "It would seem so."

"Unless he is the generous sort," Violet added.

Ruby shrugged. "Gail didn't paint that picture. Maybe he forgot what was in them."

"His loss is our gain," Violet said, finishing her muffin in record time. "Although to be fair, I've only seen this book and I haven't worked out the value. I'll need to do some research."

Ruby saw the gleam in Violet's eyes and understood it. Research gave them both so much pleasure. Especially, when it turned up interesting and occasionally obscure information. "Depending on what you find, I need to work out what to keep and what we don't need."

"Are you going to hand this over to Nate?" Scarlett pointed at the note.

"I thought I should." Ruby tilted her head. "Although, what our sheriff could do about it after all this time, I can't imagine."

"At least once you put it into his hands you won't have to wonder about it anymore," Violet noted.

Ruby frowned. "I suppose so, but aren't you even a little curious? I know I am."

"Arrgh!" Save me from curious sisters," Violet teased.

"I do believe our last adventure was when you got yourself in the middle of a theft investigation," Scarlett reminded her dryly.

"What was I supposed to do when the mayor asked me for help?"

"Not chase criminals down Main Street would have been a good place to start."

"Oh, please," Ruby interjected. "You two are both as bad as me for putting ourselves in danger."

The sisters grinned at each other. It was the truth so there was no sense denying it. Trouble found the Finch sisters with regularity. Fortunately, this time there was no body.

Yet.

Chapter Three

Ruby had two classes arrive from the local school and was kept busy, but as soon as they left, she couldn't help returning to her desk where the note was weighted down with the book it fell from.

In a flash of inspiration, she wondered if any more notes were wedged between the pages. She opened the book gently and flipped through it slowly. Nothing moved, but she did find something else. A rough edge.

Propping the book open with a stapler, she plucked the note by a corner and dropped it onto the back page. Her eyes bugged as she slid it gently into position. A perfect fit! The note had come from the Jane Austen book.

A tingle ran up and down her spine.

Thank goodness when Violet left with several books to research she hadn't taken this one.

"Ruby? Are you okay?"

Sheriff Nathaniel Adams stood at the library reception desk fending off Bob, who gave everyone the impression he was starved of attention. Dutifully he ruffled the fur on Bob's head while studying her face.

She hadn't heard him arrive and with no time to compose herself, carefully picked up the note and wordlessly handed it to him.

Eyes wide, he took it by the same corner and read it. A second or two later he looked back at her. "You actually want me to take this seriously?"

She gave him a measured look. "Don't you?"

"When Scarlett messaged to say you wanted to discuss a missing person, I thought she meant someone who was alive. I appreciate your concern, Ruby, but look at it. This note is years old."

"I can see that, but the call for help is pretty convincing."

"It could have been a joke or children leaving notes for each other."

Ruby pointed at the paper in his hand. "Have you ever seen a child's handwriting that elegant? And what about the wording?"

"Well, no, but if it was decades ago, it's likely that children back then were taught cursive writing and spoke differently."

"I hadn't considered that," Ruby admitted. "It is one possibility."

He sighed. "Clearly not the one you want to consider, so I guess you still want me to look into it?"

"It would put my mind at rest. Would you mind?"

"I am busy, so an old case, if that's what it is, wouldn't take precedence over more recent crimes," he warned.

Ruby got the impression he was humoring her, but she would take what she could get. "I appreciate that. I really do."

He gave her a skeptical look. "What did Scarlett and Violet say?"

"They thought it was too long ago to be sure who the author was, even if we could confirm it came from the Swanson family, but that it did bear looking into."

He sighed again. "Of course they did."

"Could we take a drive out to the Swansons' place and look around?"

Nate's eyes widened again. "Didn't you say the house had been sold?"

"That's right. According to Gail, Edgar Swanson is mostly moved out and the new owners move in soon."

He made a sound of frustration. "We can't walk around the place without a warrant, but I guess it wouldn't hurt to view the property from the road. We might have some luck if the owner's there and is happy to answer a few questions, but you'll have to wait until the weekend before I can spare the time."

"I guess it's waited this long." Ruby tipped her head. "We could take a picnic on Sunday and make a day of it."

"If Scarlett is happy to come, that would be a great idea." He waggled his eyebrows. "I assume you meant all of us?"

Chuckling, she nudged him. "As if Scarlett and Violet would be left behind. I'll check if they're available and get back to you. Now, I better get going, Alex is making me lunch."

Nate's demeanor changed instantly. He was fond of Alex and knew her fiancé was suffering. "How's he doing?"

"He's excited about finally opening next week, but terribly nervous it will be a flop and people will hate his food." Even saying it made Ruby's stomach clench.

Nate nodded. "Opening a Russian Diner in such a small town is a big call."

"That's the trouble," she agreed. "So many people think

that's the only food he'll serve, but his menu is far more extensive than that. He's limited his authentic dishes to the best ones in the hopes of easing people into it and will try more if they prove successful."

"Very wise." He grinned ruefully. "Unfortunately, we have more than our share of plain eaters in Cozy Hollow."

"My family knows all about that," Ruby snorted. "You would think Scarlett was trying to poison them whenever she tries new pastries or cakes." She winked at him. "Luckily, they all liked my fudge."

"That darn fudge is addictive." He inadvertently licked his lips.

Ruby grinned. "It sure made an impact on sales right away and continues to help keep the Cozy Diner in the black."

"So Scarlett told me." He smiled when he said her name. "You all seem very happy these days."

"Now that the Mayor is taking medication for his PTSD he's on our side instead of constantly trying to undermine us. With Alex living his dream as well, life is rosy for a change."

He waved the note at her. "Let's try to keep it that way."

Ruby gave him her best dimpled smile. "Yes, Sheriff."

He rolled his eyes though she also noticed a twinkle in them. He was a great sheriff and an even better friend. It would be so nice if Scarlett and he could find a way to get together. Unfortunately, every time it looked like they might, something got in the way.

Once he'd gone, she locked the library and hurried down to the diner, with George and Bob at her heels. When she got to the back door Boris greeted them with a deep ruff. Bob bounded around the large dog like a puppy and Boris put a paw on his back to slow him down. He quietened, looking up at his captor adoringly. George sidestepped them and stretched out in the sun.

Ruby gave Boris a pat and left her two guardians with their friend. They would wait for her no matter how long she took and that always made her feel special.

Alex was ready for her the moment she entered the kitchen. A place was set at the counter and after he kissed her quickly and ushered her to the seat, he placed a bowl of hearty stew in front of her. Crossing his arms over his apron he leaned back to watch her.

This was the worst part of their relationship. She was not a big eater and preferred her main meal in the early evening. But, as his fiancée, Ruby had to eat his dishes or run the risk of hurting his feelings or discouraging him. Something she could never do. The sooner the diner was a success, the sooner she could stop being fed like a skinny pet. Plus, she deeply regretted eating Scarlett's muffin.

Dutifully dipping a spoon into the velvety mixture, she inhaled the fragrance of herbs and spices. Her stomach rumbled and she already knew it was going to be delicious. Blowing on the spoon, aware that Alex was fidgeting nervously, she took her first mouthful. Flavors exploded in wave after wave. "Mmm."

"You like it?" He asked with a groan of apprehension.

Allowing a moment to savor it she swallowed, then grinned. "Alex, you just hit it out of the park! You really nailed it."

He blinked, shook his head, shrugged, and blew a lungful of air. "I do not understand. Is this a good or bad thing?"

Ruby still often forgot that with his work life, beginning as a teenage laborer on the Ukrainian border, and never seeing a television until he moved into his small cabin at the back of the timber company his father owned, Alex was still a novice when it came to colloquiums. "It is heaven in a bowl. So good. Fantastic. Brilliant!"

"This I understand." He beamed. "I should put it on the menu, yes?"

"Yes, yes, yes. The good people of Cozy Hollow will love it. Even the not so good!"

"Then I am happy." He waved a hand at the bowl. "Continue to eat."

Ruby truly wanted to finish the meal, but eventually had to concede defeat or make herself ill. "I love it, Alex. It's just too much."

He sighed at her apology. "I forget. You are so small. Violet would finish it."

Ruby laughed. Considered petite at 5'2", her sisters were the opposite at 5'8" and Violet had a legendary appetite. "She probably would. By the way, I'm organizing a picnic with Scarlett, Nate, and maybe Violet on Sunday if you can squeeze it in. It would only be for a few hours."

"I will have to consider this." His pained expression said it all.

"Please forget I mentioned it. I understand that the shop is your focus right now. Would you mind if I still go?"

Ruby couldn't miss the wave of relief that washed over his features.

"You are right. I would be thinking too much about the diner and would spoil the day. You should go and have some fun. You will be safe with Nate."

Apparently, she needed a protector wherever she went. Though she didn't want to agree with him about spoiling the day, perhaps she wouldn't enlighten him right away about the note and the true reason for the picnic.

Chapter Four

That Sunday Nate drove the group out of town while the sisters chatted as if they hadn't seen each other for days and the conversation mainly revolved around the Swansons.

Violet had researched the books with Ruby at night and, though many of them wouldn't be worth much, Ruby selected some classics for the library while Violet took the older ones which would sell well in her store.

"Did you tell Gail about the note?" Ruby asked.

Violet shook her head. "Not yet. I felt we should wait until after today or at least until I can find out more about the background of the estate."

"That makes sense." Scarlett nodded. "Gail's a sensitive woman who could very well freak out about the letter."

"It would be upsetting if she thinks like us, that a relative has been kept captive or harmed." Ruby agreed.

"If only the note had been more on the lines of, 'I hope whoever find this enjoys the book as much as I did.' That kinda thing would be lovely," Ruby said wistfully.

"I still think it's a joke," Nate muttered.

Scarlett gave him a side-eye from the passenger seat. "Let's keep an open mind for a while longer."

"Sure." Nate glanced back at Ruby and neatly changed the subject. "How's the giant coping with his opening tomorrow?"

"He's pretending it will all be fine, but I can tell he's petrified no one will come and if they do they'll hate his food."

"Still? The poor man. I hope he knows I'd be there if I could?" Scarlett shared her disappointment. "The cafe is busy these days, which I can hardly complain about."

"Don't worry, Alex knows his friends will be there in spirit if they can't make it, and I'm sure there will be plenty of interested or curious customers. Besides, people are getting used to me closing the library for half an hour at lunch time. I'll check on him then."

"You do have to have a break some time," Violet stated.

"I've begun to appreciate that. In the beginning, I was just so delighted to get the librarian's job, that in the beginning I didn't mind eating my lunch or fitting a break in when I could. However, it can be a little awkward at times." Ruby blushed feeling disloyal to the job she loved. "Plus, we're getting busier as the community grows and more people come across from Harmony Beach. I've got my fingers and toes crossed that at the next town meeting funds get passed for a part-timer."

"That's a great idea. Good luck getting money from the mayor though," Scarlett teased.

"If anyone can get money out of him, it's Ruby." Violet laughed. "She's his favorite resident."

"Stop that," Ruby said without conviction.

In truth, she did share a bond with Arthur Tully, but so did all the Finch women. The mayor had been in love with their mother and would have done anything for Lilac Finch. Unfortunately, when his PTSD kicked in after her death, he couldn't bear to see Lilac's daughters as they reminded him of her. He'd attempted to get them to leave town by causing the bakery to fail through misinformation and gossip. When that didn't happen, he was forced into facing the truth by Ruby.

Once he got diagnosed and put on meds he was a different man, but he had never been as mean to Ruby as he had to the others, and she'd found it easy to forgive him. Her sisters had taken a while longer, but eventually they put it behind them. On the other hand, Arthur seemed bent on making up for his horrid behavior and couldn't do enough for them—Ruby in particular. If she could get some help at the library she would be in his debt again, but this time she didn't feel guilty for using her connections. Yes, she could have her breaks, but another librarian would benefit the whole community. There would be no need to close the library if she were sick or when she finally took time off for a honeymoon.

Just thinking about that made her skin tingle. "Besides," Ruby continued with a smirk, "having a sister on the committee should help get it over the line."

Scarlett winked. "You know I'll vote for it. The library is important to the town and having a librarian who is so good at bringing the communities together, is worth funding an assistant to ensure that continues."

Violet groaned and made a gagging sound.

Scarlett reached a long finger back and poked her sister. "You know it's true, Vi."

Violet snorted. "Whatever."

"I knew I could count on you, Scarlett. Just as I know that underneath her denial, Violet thinks I'm awesome."

Ruby giggled and decided this was the perfect opportunity to mention Alex's suggestion. "By the way, I was having a poor me moment about missing baking..."

"What?" Scarlett scoffed. "You don't like to bake."

Ruby gaped for a moment. "Since when?"

"Since you left the café to be a librarian."

"Even before that," Violet agreed.

Ruby was a little offended. "I understand why you might think that, because I might not have been so happy about it at the time, but I had a plan. In fact, we all had the same plan for me, right?"

Scarlett and Violet shared a contemplative look.

"The kid is right," Violet admitted reluctantly.

Scarlett merely nodded, so Ruby forged ahead. "Anyway, when you've both finished spoiling the moment, I was telling Alex how I felt and he came up with the perfect solution."

"Which is?" Violet asked warily.

"Well, I don't know if you'll be keen, Vi, but Alex suggested that we bake together each morning. Just for an hour or so," she added the last bit hurriedly when Violet almost choked. "Don't you think it would be nice to bake and chat like we used to?"

Scarlett's eyes misted. "Mom would love it and an hour's help would set the café up for the day. It would also mean that Aunt Olivia wouldn't have to get up so early."

"Ughh! You two," Violet groaned. "Fine. I'll give it a try, but you know I hate mornings."

"We know," the other two chorused.

From the driver's seat, Nate smothered a laugh with a cough.

The drive to the picnic continued to be almost festive, despite the reason for it. When they arrived, Nate parked on the side of a small hill opposite the Swansons' land. He had googled it to make sure they had the right place, but it would be hard to miss since from Cozy Hollow to Harmony Beach there was nothing else like it. They climbed to the top of the hill which boasted a large flat area and afforded them a birds eye view of the estate.

"It must have been magnificent once," Scarlett said wistfully.

"It still is," Violet asserted. "Even in its admittedly shabby state and having had most of the land sold off. Imagine the cost of trying to keep everything in perfect condition. I know when Mayor Tully talked about his renovations he said they cost an arm and a leg. The Swanson Estate is far larger and older."

"You're right, Vi. It's still gorgeous." Ruby pointed to the east of the house. "Look. It has its own graveyard. I'd love to get a closer look."

Scarlett's eyebrows shot up. "You want to look at a graveyard?"

"I admit it wouldn't be my favorite past time normally, but what if our note writer is buried there?"

Violet snorted. "And how on earth would we know who to look for, when we don't have a name?"

"That's mostly true." With a flourish, Ruby pulled a piece of paper from her bag. "I did a little research on the genealogy of the family and came up with a list of names."

Nate took the paper from her and scanned the list. "You do understand that pinning the graves down to anyone on this list will be like the proverbial needle in a haystack?"

Ruby nodded and pulled out the book she had found the note in. She removed the protective cloth she had wrapped it in and flicked to the back of the book. "Violet and I discussed the fact that the paper is as old as the book and when I looked closer, I found that a page has been torn out here."

"You'd never notice if you weren't looking for it." Violet gave Ruby a questioning look. "If I may?"

"Go ahead," Ruby said with increasing excitement.

Violet took a deep breath. "The paper is old and matches that used in the book. The ripped edges also line up with each other, so we can surmise that the note did come from this book. The handwriting is old school, which points to that of an older person, or someone taught to write this way. Perhaps a younger person who was home-schooled. The pen used is just that, a pen. Not a fountain pen, as we might assume would have been used by an older person at that time."

"What do you mean by that time?" Nate asked. "How do you gauge that?"

Ruby took charge again. "In the front of the book there is always a date of publication. As you can see on the page opposite, there is a dedication—in fountain pen. Violet spotted that."

Scarlett turned to their middle sister and smiled fondly. "Your training with Phin certainly gave you new and varied skills."

"I like to think so," Violet said matter-of-factly. "Qualifying as an assessor has proven invaluable with my store, which I never would have opened if it hadn't been for Phin's encouragement, and his tutoring. While not being wholly definitive, this is one example of reaching a conclusion. Sometimes it's the best we can hope for when judging the value of something."

Ruby and Scarlett accepted that Violet wasn't showing off. A renowned assessor for many years, Phineas Jacobs had taken Violet under his wing when she showed an inclination for his passion. This had come about when together they solved an odd murder involving another old book.

They got on so well he was now a silent partner in her antiques business. Although, that might be less of a reason than the fact that he had taken a liking for their Aunt Olivia who worked in the café with Scarlett. His foot in the business provided the perfect excuse to come back to Cozy Hollow—often.

Nate coughed. "When you lot are done, can we at least sit down and eat whatever smells so good?"

Chapter Five

Ruby shook the blanket she carried and spread it on the ground. Scarlett had packed a large hamper and Nate placed it on one corner of the blanket to prevent the breeze from blowing it down the hill.

Violet put a large flask of coffee beside it and they took a seat admiring the view while Scarlett emptied the hamper. She handed out plates and napkins while the others removed lids.

Nate smacked his lips. "It was worth the drive just for this feast."

Scarlett smiled at him and the look they shared before she took a coffee cup from Violet, made Ruby's insides gooey. She made a mental note to speak to Violet about how to get the two of them to commit to each other and put aside the baggage they carried.

Bursting at the seams to get to the sleuthing, she waited with a veneer of patience until everyone had eaten at least one thing before pressing for a decision. Swallowing a bite of delicious chicken salad sandwich, she looked at them expectantly. "So, when we're done here, what shall we do first?"

"We should go to the front door and announce our presence," Nate told them firmly.

"I guess that would be polite. What will we say?"

"Well, for starters we won't say we're looking for a dead person."

"No. Let's not do that." Ruby continued to smile, though it was hard to remain calm. "Should we show them the note?"

"I think it best to play it by ear." Violet waved a slice of ham and egg pie at her. "If the owner isn't happy to have us on his land then it wouldn't be a good idea to show all our cards in one go in case we need to sneak back in."

"Our cards? Sneaking?" Nate growled. "Look, nobody is to get carried away. I don't have any answers for the correct procedure in something so flimsy it's probably a big fat nothing, but I am not trespassing."

"Nobody is asking you to," Scarlett pointed out. "You can wait in the car."

Nate growled again. "None of us are trespassing. End of story."

"All right. No need to get testy," Violet huffed.

Scarlett refilled their cups. "It's such a shame that Alex couldn't make it. He loves the countryside."

The way her eldest sister diffused the situation by changing the subject was smart and gave Nate time to cool down.

"He does," Ruby said pleasantly and gazed around her, though her focus was firmly on the house across the road. No matter that Nate was probably right about the whole trespassing thing, she couldn't shake the feeling that the note was too important not to pursue it. But how could she do that with him around? Should she have come here on her own? Along with Nate, Alex would have been furious and receiving a lecture from either of them didn't excite her. She took a thoughtful sip of coffee, deciding all wasn't lost yet.

Willing them to hurry and finish their lunch, and unable to sit still another minute, she stood and walked around the vantage point. The view was 360 degrees of idyllic valley bathed in sunlight. There were a few farm houses here and there, but largely the area was uninhabited. Unless you counted cows, chickens, and alpacas.

Nothing moved around the large house across the road and many of the curtains were closed. A substantial driveway curved around the front and continued to the back.

"I'd love to get a look inside the place. I bet there will be some antiques left behind. Not everyone understands the value of old furniture and memorabilia and I'd hate to think they would get thrown out as trash."

Ruby turned to Violet who now stood beside her. "It might be worth a look inside, but no matter what Nate says. I am going to the graveyard."

Violet clutched her chest. "Ohhh, listen to you being brave and determined."

Ruby waggled a finger in her face. "I mean it. If we can't do it today, then I'll come back on my own."

"Alex would have a fit," Violet said reasonably.

"Alex doesn't have to know everything."

Violet dodged the finger for a second time. "He is your fiancé, but if you're not going to let him in on your mission, then you better tell me when you're going rogue and I'll come." Suddenly she gripped Ruby's finger. "Do not come out here on your own. Okay?"

Ridiculously grateful for the forceful support, Ruby

leaned in and hugged her. "Thanks, Vi. I'd appreciate having you with me."

Violet shrugged her off. "I could hardly let my kid sister walk into potential danger on her own."

"You never have. Besides, you want to know if this is real or a hoax just as much as me, right?"

Violet shrugged again. "Of course I do, and as much as she's trying to appease Nate, I bet you a batch of chocolate muffins that Scarlett does too."

They grinned at each other, and Ruby grabbed her arm.

"Come on. They must be finished eating and making cow eyes at each other by now. Maybe we're over-thinking this and the owner will let us look to our hearts content."

"He may, but you still need to think of a reason for wanting to look around."

Ruby blinked. "Darn it. I'd overlooked that little issue."

"Now I can see how bad you want to know who wrote the note. You never forget things," Violet observed.

When they returned to where they'd left the couple, all traces of the picnic were cleared away and they were already on their way back to the car with the hamper. Scarlett walked beside Nate, head tilted and laughing at something he said.

"They should have gone on their own picnic," Ruby stated. "It can't be very romantic having your girlfriend's sisters watching your every move."

"What move is that?" Violet's voice was heavy with sarcasm. "He's so proper, if we don't intervene, I doubt the two of them will ever make anything happen."

This played right into Ruby's hands. "You're right Vi, and I accept the challenge."

Giggling like teenagers instead of women in their mid-twenties, they linked arms and ran down the hill to arrive breathless at the car.

"The fresh air seems to have done you some good," Nate said approvingly to Ruby.

She guessed he meant her irritation at him playing everything by the book had shown, which she had already decided was unfair of her. A sheriff had to do what he had to do—and so did a Finch woman. "I do feel better," she acknowledged. "Shall we go see if anyone is home?"

Nate insisted on driving the short distance so that the occupant might see them coming and not be worried about a group turning up on his doorstep unannounced. They piled out again in front of the large main door and Nate knocked on the weathered oak. They waited for a couple of minutes which seemed much longer to Ruby, then he knocked again. No one came.

"What now?" Nate asked.

"Let's walk around the back," Ruby suggested. "It's a big house and if they are outside they might not have heard the knocking."

Nate gave her a side-eye, but nodded and led them down the path. Weeds grew amongst the gravel and choked the plants in the window boxes. By the unkempt looks of them, the trees hadn't had a trim in years. All the windows had a film of grime and the chimney they passed was cracked from top to bottom.

"How sad," whispered Scarlett.

Ruby nodded, though her attention was on the grave-yard which she could see on the small hill in the distance. Around the corner they came across a long terrace with steps leading down to a large level lawn. "I bet they played croquet out here once. Like Alice in Wonderland."

"Your imagination never fails to impress me," Nate said with a shake of his head. "I'll knock at the back door."

There were in fact, several doors along this side of the house and most were glass. The first was a set of double doors that led into a large conservatory and the second looked like it housed the sitting room. From where they stood the rooms looked almost empty, but there was at least one overstuffed chair in that one which presumably meant it was still in use.

Nate climbed the cracked steps and lifted his hand to knock when a gruff question made him pause.

"Who are you and what are you doing on my land?"

A short round man dressed in a tweed jacket and brown trousers with a cap on his head stood behind them. A shot gun rested across both forearms. He looked and sounded like he should be in the English countryside instead of Oregon.

"Mr. Swanson?" Nate asked.

"Who wants to know?"

"I'm Sheriff Adams from Cozy Hollow."

The man looked down an aristocratic nose. "Since you are not in uniform, should I take your word for it?"

Nate pulled out his badge. "Sorry, I'm actually not working today and this is not official business."

The man came closer and peered at the badge making Ruby suspect he usually wore glasses for reading.

"Then please explain why you are on private property if you are not on police business?"

Nate nodded at Ruby. "My friend, Ruby Finch, received a box of books from your cousin, Gail Norman."

The man's eyes narrowed. "She gave them away?"

"Ruby runs the Cozy Hollow library and Mrs. Norman thought the town might benefit from them."

Mr. Swanson considered this for a moment. "Well, since they were given to Gail, I guess what she does with them is none of my business. In which case I am still at a loss to understand what the problem is that would bring you here unannounced."

"There is no problem, Sir." Violet stepped forward. "My sister merely wanted to check the authenticity of the books so that she could promote them as original works."

His eyes lit up. "Are you saying they are worth a lot of money?"

Violet wrinkled her nose. "Not necessarily, but it would be nice to know how long they had been in the family and whose collection it was."

"And you needed the sheriff to find that out?" he scoffed.

Scarlett gave a cheery little laugh. "The sheriff is a family friend and only here because we had a picnic on the hill across the road. It has a wonderful view as I'm sure you must know and it got us thinking that as we were here we could ask you in person since Gail didn't seem to know."

He gave her a skeptical look. "All I can tell you is that the books have been in this house my whole life and my mother was the owner of everything you see until the day she died."

Ruby detected more than a little annoyance in the statement, but was this directed at them or his mother? "This place is amazing. I believe you sold some of the land at an earlier date. How much of the surrounding pastures come with the house now?"

He grunted. "The property extends to the tallest tree line on three sides. But, if you're looking to buy, it's already been sold."

"We did hear that it was sold. I'm sure you will miss living in such lovely surroundings."

He sighed heavily. "I won't miss the work or the cost of maintaining it. The place is too big for one person to manage."

Up close, the estate was even more rundown than she had thought and Ruby could imagine his frustration at seeing it worsen year by year. "We know how that feels," she empathized. "We've been through a similar experience when our mom passed away. It was on a much less grand scale, but still hard not having the money to fix things. I suppose the property was sold with the graveyard?"

He seemed to be perplexed by her story and the question as he nodded shortly. "Of course. Why do you ask?"

"I was thinking of all the family and memories there must be up there." Ruby nodded pointedly toward the graveyard.

He stiffened. "Except for my father who I wasn't close to, the people buried there were mostly long gone before I could remember them and my mother is buried in the town cemetery."

Was Mrs. Swanson's burial place simply good foresight if he was already considering selling? Or something more sinister?

Chapter Six

"Since we're here, would you mind if we took a look around the grounds?" Ruby asked brightly when she realized he was staring at her.

Edgar Swanson blinked. "If you want information on the books, why are you so interested in my land?"

"It's not about the land, Mr. Swanson. My sister, Violet, is an assessor and loves looking at old things, including buildings. We don't have much of this vintage in Cozy Hollow and you never know, she might spot something of value you had over-looked."

His eyes brightened at that, but it didn't last long. "I'm busy clearing out the house, but I guess it can't hurt to look around the place, if you stay out of the barn. The roof is apparently not safe." He grimaced. "The new owners wrangled the price down because of it." He didn't look pleased at all about that.

"Thank you so much," Ruby smiled as sweetly as she could. "Come on, Violet." She linked arms again and pulled her sister in the direction of the outbuildings where a selection of ancient machinery sat around gathering rust.

Nate and Scarlett followed slowly behind them and Ruby checked over her shoulder several times before scampering behind the closest building. From here she made a beeline for the graveyard. She heard Violet muttering and then her footsteps close behind her.

When they got to the picket fence surrounding the graves, Ruby looked back once more. Since the ground rose slightly, they were hidden from the yard by the outer buildings, but not the house itself. She walked casually around the picket fence that was falling down in many places and bent to pick a handful of wildflowers. Next she carefully stepped over some fallen palings and was in the graveyard. At the closest grave she laid several flowers.

Violet leaned against a post and snorted. "As much as I know how soft-hearted you are, you don't know these people. So what are you really doing?"

"If Mr. Swanson's watching, I want him to think I'm paying my respects and not snooping to see who is buried here."

"Oh. Good idea." Violet picked her own flowers and followed suit. "Look at this grave. I think it says, 'Amelia'. She died 48 years ago."

"Edgar must have been a teenager at the time of her death, which doesn't marry with him saying he wouldn't know any of the people buried here." Ruby knelt at another cross close by. "This one was also 48 years ago, but I can't read the name. Maybe they were twins!"

Violet tutted. "That would be even more devastating than losing one child. It's odd that there isn't a surname."

Ruby studied each cross again. "You're right. Why would that be if they were Edgar's siblings? And what did they die of? Medicine has come a long way in 48 years and I know it can't change things, but I wonder if they could have been saved with better knowledge."

"Probably. It could have been anything. I bet it would say something on their medical records." Violet looked back at the house. "It's a shame we can't get access."

"We could try the obituaries?" Ruby suggested.

"I thought you'd already researched them?"

"I have, but I didn't know what I was looking for. Twins might be easier to find. I just wish we knew who the mother and father were."

Violet pointed at a large headstone. This one says Robert Swanson. Must be Edgar's father. The ones behind are quite ornate."

Ruby squinted at the faded names. "They must be his parents. I wonder exactly where Edgar's mother is buried."

"He said in town which must mean the cemetery by the church."

"How's it going?" Nate asked when he and Scarlett got close enough not to shout.

Ruby saw they held hands and when she caught Scarlett's eye her sister shrugged.

"Don't get carried away. It's a cover for your nefarious act," Scarlett told her airily.

"Ah huh." Violet winked at Ruby.

She grinned and glanced one last time over the small graveyard that held the history for an entire family over decades. Something caught her eye as she was leaving. "What's that?" She pointed to a piece of wood stuck in the ground at the back of the plot. Ruby picked her way through the broken bits of headstone and weeds. "It's a broken cross!"

"Is there a name?" Violet called.

Ruby shook her head. "It's just two bits of wood that have been nailed together."

"It could be a pet," Nate said reasonably.

"In the family graveyard?" Violet asked.

Scarlett tilted her head. "If we had one, wouldn't we put George and Bob in it?"

"I see your point," Violet conceded. "They are our family, aren't they?"

"Of course they are," Ruby agreed. "More importantly, they chose us."

"As delightful as this conversation is, Edgar Swanson is out on his veranda and looking this way," Nate warned.

"Let's walk back casually and give him a wave," Scarlett suggested. "After all he was kind enough to give his permission to walk around his property. A man with something to hide wouldn't have done that."

"He's very grumpy, even though he did agree," Violet grumbled.

Scarlett tutted. "Anyone would be if they had to sell the family home that they'd lived in all their lives."

Ruby heard the tone that suggested they needed to be more reasonable about this and sighed. "You're right. I could be looking for something that simply isn't there."

"I'm glad you can see that possibility," Scarlett said gently. "Maybe in a few days, when you're shattered from getting up early to bake and working all day, you'll find that your imagination got the better of you."

Ruby sighed again. She honestly didn't think she was so desperate for a mystery that she'd grasped at the note the way Scarlett was alluding to. Nate was watching the exchange closely and she considered that he had talked her sister into putting the whole thing down to Ruby being fanciful. Which was something else to get her head around, but not right now.

So, what did she want to find? Someone she could help? Was there a flaw in her make-up that made her want to be needed? The person who wrote this note was likely deceased and it wasn't as if she didn't have plenty to keep her mind occupied. The library and Alex's diner saw to that.

And yet...

Chapter Seven

According to the weather forecast, Monday promised sunshine. Regardless of that, as usual Ruby was optimistic for a great week ahead.

It was opening day at the diner and she was pretty sure that poor Alex hadn't got a bit of sleep last night. He'd called her several times during the evening worried about silly things that had magnified in his head until he was certain any one of them would make his venture a disaster. She'd talked him down each time and finally he stopped calling long enough for her to get some sleep. Ruby suspected it was only because he felt bad for keeping her up and not due to being any calmer.

Rising early, she helped get things ready to take to the café then informed her sisters she wouldn't be joining them as she was too exhausted. What she really wanted was to check on Alex and, if time permitted, to investigate the letter some more.

Violet would have none of her excuses and practically dragged her out the door. "It was your idea, Ruby Finch, and I did not get up extra early to do this without you suffering alongside me."

Yawning through making muffins, Ruby wasn't entirely surprised when Alex peered through the kitchen window. She beckoned him in and when she saw how pale he was she rushed to hug him.

"You're covered in flour," Violet chuckled. "And now so is he."

Ruby made to pull away, but Alex held on tight for a while longer.

"I do not care," he whispered into her hair.

Scarlett held out a steaming coffee mug and a fresh muffin. "Alex, I forbid you to be nervous today. It won't help anything and you know we love your cooking; therefore it must be good. Now, when you've finished that, you need to get over to your diner and open for breakfast. It would not be a good look to be late on the first day."

"Do you need me to help with anything?" Ruby asked, annoyed with herself for not instinctively going straight to the diner, despite him saying he was fine the last time they spoke about it.

He nodded while his eyes pierced her heart. "Everything is set up and I will go very soon. I just needed..."

"A hug," Violet finished for him and put her arms around his back. Scarlett joined the huddle from the side and Alex made a rumbling sound in his chest.

The three women leaned back, relieved he was chuckling and not crying. No one outside of them, his sister, and Nate would know that Alex was such a sensitive soul.

"That is exactly what I needed. I will see you at lunch, Ruby." He kissed her tenderly and the other sisters backed away to give them room.

"We'll be there at some stage depending on customers," Scarlett assured him.

He nodded and bustled out the door.

"Poor baby," Violet teased, but her mouth wobbled.

"If he concentrates on his food and lets Lexie organize the customers, he'll be fine," Scarlett assured them. "Now you both need to get to your real jobs, but thanks for the help. Aunt Olivia will be here any minute, and she asked me to tell you thanks for letting her take a later start."

Their aunt was their mother's sister. She'd been almost a second mom to the girls growing up and more so after their mom's death. She had even sold part of her craft store to Gail Norman so she could come help Scarlett. Violet took another share of the store and along with Phineas, had added antiques to it. The new and old merged into a beautiful space and Violet was rightly proud of it.

Their lives had indeed changed and yet they were as close as ever. The hum of the kitchen as they worked this morning had proved that. Maybe it wouldn't continue forever, this early morning togetherness, but for now it was important to Ruby and she could tell that despite her protestations, Violet enjoyed it too. Naturally, it was a big help to Scarlett who showed her gratitude by making sure they had a decent breakfast and took something nice for lunch.

Family was important to Ruby, her sisters, and to Alex. Though Alex's upbringing had been tough he wanted the same thing as she did—to belong. It took years for her to understand that not everyone felt the same way. These thoughts brough her mind back to the note, making her wonder how Agatha Swanson felt about her family and how it had shaped Edgar?

When she had a few spare minutes she went online and

looked up the local paper. They had quite a lot of back issues available so she searched for anything on the Swansons.

The first thing that came up was Agatha's death. It was just a brief obituary to say she had died at home peacefully. There was another about Robert's death many years earlier and in between there was an article about land from the estate being sold to an adjacent farmer. The family were mentioned in several places as having attended events in the area, but nothing recently. Ruby discovered that there had not been a local paper any earlier so if she wanted more she would have to dig through other archives. The thought appealed, but she didn't have the time right now.

Arriving at the diner just after midday, Ruby found Alex standing right inside the front door welcoming everyone, even though his sister was willing and able to do the job she had signed on for. He gave Ruby a wonky grin that hid none of his anguish and sweat beaded his forehead as he hurried to the kitchen to fill orders.

Lexie sighed. "He's been like this since the minute we opened and if anything it's gotten worse. If he's not careful, he's going to give himself a heart attack."

Ruby clasped her shoulder. "Once today is done and he sees how much people love his food, he'll calm down."

"You have no idea how much I'm relying on that." Lexie sighed. "I feel like he's dragging me into his pit of unworthiness and I'm sure I'll wind up saying stupid things."

Ruby smiled encouragingly. "Looking the way you do,

and with your gentle voice, there's no way anyone will think you don't have everything in hand."

Lexie beamed at her. "I'm so glad you're going to be my sister-in-law. Everyone should have a Ruby in their corner."

The women's laughter died as Leona Wolf came in the door. Her nose was in the air as she sniffed loudly and gave the place a long look.

"Good afternoon. Welcome to Alex's Diner," Lexie crooned.

"Well that's the first mistake in my book. Why isn't it called the Cozy Diner?" she demanded.

Ruby and Lexie shared a grimace. It wasn't the first query either of them had had over the name. The whole town had jumped on the cozy theme when years ago the town committee suggested a theme. Now all the stores had cozy in their name including the Cozy Café.

"Alex isn't from Cozy Hollow," Ruby reminded her. "And if you recall, before the diner burned down, that was the name. Alex doesn't want to be associated with that trouble."

Leona sniffed. "I recall it very well, but if he wants to be thought of as one of us he really should have considered that not using cozy in the name would have the opposite effect."

"May I show you to your seat?" Lexie asked as politely as her gritted teeth, pretending to be a smile, would allow.

"I suppose I should try something, otherwise I can hardly rate the food."

"That is very true," Ruby said. "Alex has worked so hard on the menu, I'm sure you'll find a dish to your taste."

"We'll see. I don't hold with foreign food as a rule, but you know how I like to give people a chance."

The two women shot each other another glance as

Lexie ushered Leona to a table by the window, away from the kitchen and not too near the door.

Ruby nodded to herself. There was no doubt that model looks aside, Lexie was a great asset for the business. Over the high counter, which separated the kitchen and the diner, Alex patted a bell and placed a plate of steak and fries on the counter under heat lamps.

Lexi handed Leona a menu then hurried to collect the waiting food and deliver it with a flourish along with cutlery and napkins. The customer was Dale Wilkens from Cozy Cars and he immediately tucked in, while Alex watched from the kitchen. Dale gave him a thumb up and finally Alex smiled. He beckoned to Ruby and put a smaller plate on the counter.

"This is for you."

"Oh, you shouldn't have bothered."

"You must eat." He stated this as if she were in the habit of starving herself which would be impossible when Scarlett was such an awesome baker and she and Violet were hardly slouches when it came to cooking.

She took the plate graciously. "Thank you. I am hungry."

"If you need more, I will bring it."

"I won't. This is the perfect amount," she assured him, wondering how she could change his definition of portion size.

"I remembered what you said," he told her proudly, as if loading a smaller plate until it groaned was the same thing as a small portion.

She blew him a kiss and Lexie showed her to a corner table.

"Is this okay?"

"Of course it is. I don't need special treatment."

"Hah! Even if I didn't think you deserved it, which you do, Alex would have a fit if I treated you like everyone else. In case you didn't notice, my big brother is crazy over you."

Ruby blushed. "I feel the same way about him."

"Really? Tell me something I don't know." Chuckling, Lexie breezed away to collect another order from the pass.

Ruby glanced around the room. Everything sparkled with newness and the smells from the kitchen were heavenly. Just as she predicted, the diner was going to be fine—if people like Leona gave it a chance.

She glanced across the room and noted that Leona was looking her way as if studying her. The woman quickly gave her attention back to her menu. Sure that it wasn't a casual meeting of eyes across a room, this reaction made Ruby curious.

Leona was born and bred in Cozy Hollow. She knew everyone in town and nearby. If she didn't, she found out about them. Could it be that the Swanson estate was part of her—realm?

Chapter Eight

That afternoon, Violet burst into the library with a book tucked under her arm. Bob growled until he saw who it was and George raced to her side beating Bob for the first pat.

"Where's the fire?" Ruby asked.

After a cursory pat and scratch for both, Violet carefully pushed through the fur and paws. "You won't believe it. I found another note."

Ruby gasped. "Show me!"

Removing the paper from the book Violet placed it carefully on the library counter.

Help me!

I must get free for the sake of my children.

Ruby reached under the counter and pulled out the first book and a copy of the original note, grateful that she had the foresight to make one. She placed the copy beside Violet's.

They leaned down to compare the two, heads almost touching, and Violet gasped.

"Same handwriting!"

"I think so too. She was frightened." Ruby pointed out that the writing had a slightly erratic style to it, as if the author's hand shook.

Violet nodded vigorously "I agree that the author must be a woman."

"It does hint at it, though we can't be sure." Ruby gulped, feeling she had to say this, while in her mind she was certain, and it wasn't only to do with the handwriting. "Do you think she's the mother of the babies buried up in the graveyard?"

Violet frowned. "That's a possibility. Let's think about how old this person might be. The ballpoint pen was invented in 1888 and introduced to the United States around 1939 to 1940. Therefore the notes had to have been written after that, which is quite a large time span, but one we might be able to narrow down. Did you happen to see what the birthdates on the headstones said?"

"Now that you ask, I realize there weren't any—only the date of their death." Ruby shrugged. "I assumed they died young because of the size of the graves."

"Me too. It's odd that there is no birth date on them when every other grave had both." Violet tilted her head. "Although, there was also that random cross on its own. I know you've checked online, but if there wasn't anything obvious, then we need to look at the county birth and death records."

Ruby nodded slowly as she considered what she did know and appreciated it wasn't enough to make any informed guess. "We'd have to go to Destiny unless they hold them at the church. That is possible."

"Then let's try the church first." Violet impatiently brushed a strand of hair from her face, "Is it wrong that I'm excited about this?"

"I'm not sure, but I feel the same way," Ruby admitted. "Even if we're too late to save her or the babies, we might be able to solve the mystery and help her rest in peace."

Violet rolled her eyes. "Sheesh. You've written a whole story for this woman, haven't you?"

Ruby looked away guiltily. "Is it that obvious?"

"Transparently. Shall we go to the church after work."

"I was just about to suggest that and perhaps we should hang onto this note for a little longer?"

They grinned at each other and Violet left with her book. Nate still had the first note, and Ruby was glad that she and Violet were on the same page. They might need it to verify the penmanship—if they could find out who fit the time frame and on the off chance they had left behind any documents written or signed by them.

So many ifs and likely many reasons why they wouldn't find out who wrote those letters, but having the odds stacked against them couldn't faze a Finch woman too much.

The church was over a hundred years old and sat at the very edge of town on the way to Destiny. Minister Ambrose Chandler had been there for decades, was hard of hearing, and could be blunt to the point of rudeness. The Finch sisters didn't have a great deal to do with him by choice and had heard from their aunt that he was due to retire.

"Please let me do the talking, Vi," Ruby pleaded. "We need to sweet talk him and not try to bulldoze the man into hunting out old records."

Violet snorted. "I should be upset about that, but we both know I'm likely to offend the sanctimonious..."

"Vi!" Ruby hissed.

The minister stood at his pulpit shouting at the empty church. Empty except for Violet and Ruby. When he looked up and saw his audience he stopped mid-rant.

"Good evening," Ruby said as they walked up the aisle.

"Good evening ladies. What brings you to church for this rare visit?" His tone suggested this was an anomaly he wasn't happy about.

"We're so sorry to bother you, but we'd like to look at some birth and death records? It's for a project we're working on."

His eyebrows knitted together. "I haven't heard of any town projects."

Ruby shrugged casually, hoping her warming cheeks didn't give her away. "It's a very new thing for the library and not common knowledge yet."

"And the nature of this "project" is?" he asked in a voice laden with suspicion.

"It's all about the history of our residents and where our forebearers came from. It was something our mom was passionate about."

Violet didn't so much as blink at Ruby's exaggeration, and seemed to be impressed by her sister's imagination and the speed with which she came up with the excuse. Everyone had loved Lilac Finch, but that didn't stop Ruby feeling odd about using their mom as a carrot.

The minister nodded sagely. "Your mother was a pillar of the community and we all mourn her loss. I commend you for the effort of keeping her memory alive through this project." He paused and nodded once more. "Keeping history alive, so that our young people do not take for granted what their ancestors achieved, through much toil and hardship, would be a good sermon."

"Thank you and I totally agree," Ruby gushed. "History is one of the reasons I became a librarian. Books can be such a comfort. Don't you think?"

"They do have a place in my heart Ms. Finch, but the church is obviously the best comfort of all."

Ruby nodded. "Of course."

He gave her a skeptical glance perhaps recalling that the Finch women were not regular attendees. "So you'd like to look at my records?"

Though she would have loved to contest the ownership of those records and could feel Violet's animosity building from beside her, she smiled. "Yes, please. If you don't mind?"

"I was practicing for Sunday, but I can come back to it."

"Please don't let us stop you from what is promising to be a rousing sermon. If you show us where we can peruse them, we'll leave you to it."

Glancing somewhat wistfully at the pulpit and his nest of papers on top of it, the minister hesitated and eyed them warily.

"We would be very careful and certainly wouldn't remove anything," Ruby assured him.

"I should hope not," he said gravely. "Please follow me." He led them through a curtain at the side of the room and into a small hallway. Indicating they proceed him into a room on the left, they entered a large office.

Violet stilled in the middle of the room. "These cabinets are amazing," she gasped. "They're from the turn of the 19th century."

The minister beamed. "Very good, Ms. Finch. I see you have learned your trade well."

"Thank you," she said sincerely. "I love every piece of furniture in this room. I am in heav... I mean I'm so privileged to see such things of beauty which have been so well cared for they look new."

The smile was replaced by the minister's usual frown. He had clearly appreciated what Violet intended to say. "They are mere possessions and their monetary value means nothing to me."

"Of course not, but their beauty can still be admired. Like a painting, or a flower."

He nodded slowly. "Yes. That is very true. I am at peace in this room and I think much of that is the warmth of the furniture which emanates from its history. Now, let me get you the records. How far back did you say you wanted?"

Ruby hadn't said any time frame, but it came to her that they might not get another chance, so the wider their net, the better. "The last hundred years would be fantastic."

He ran his hands along a shelve of large books and pulled out two of them, laying them on his desk. He tapped the first one. "Please be extra careful with this one. It is the oldest and the most fragile."

"We will." Ruby promised. "Thank you so much."

"If you need me, I will be in the church." With a barely concealed frown he left the room, leaving the door open."

Violet smirked. "Trusting soul, isn't he?"

"Shush. He might hear you." Ruby crept to the door to ensure he wasn't lurking nearby. The hall was empty and she hurried back to the desk. "Let's take a book each to save time."

Chapter Nine

Ruby turned page after page, running her finger down the names. Luckily, the writing was legible and the column of surnames featured first.

The Swansons showed up halfway through the book. A Tobias Swanson possibly owned the land as far back as the 1800's. She would need to look at land records after this to be sure, but the address was the same one as the place they had visited. Tobias was listed as an immigrant from Holland and he married Fanny Pankett in 1878. Fanny was from Kent, England. They had four children. Manfred, Lester, Emilia, and Ingrid. Both girls died as babies. Manfred married Edith Lincoln in 1899 and had a son, Charlie in 1902. Charlie married Lottie Smith in 1922 and they had a son, Robert, in 1933. Lester married Dorothy Miller in 1901 but he and his wife died in a train crash on their honeymoon.

At the end of the first book, Ruby leaned over to show the notes she had taken on her phone to Violet.

"Excellent. After the death of Robert's parents is when things get interesting. Robert married Agatha Denton in

1960. He was 27 and she was only 18. They had a son, Edgar in 1961."

"That's our Edgar." Ruby tapped the page.

Violet snorted. "I imagine it is."

Ruby nudged her. "What I mean is, we are up to date. They are the last of the line according to this. Yet, it says nothing of children being born to any of them. which is odd when you consider the graves."

Violet blinked and flicked a couple of pages back and forth. "After the death of Robert Swanson in 1973, there are no more records for the family until Agatha's death a few months ago, so I think we can safely say that Edgar is the last of the Swansons. However, I did find the birth record for Meredith Denton. She was born in 1958. That is a big age difference between the sisters. Also their mother died in 1958 - the same year Meredith was born, and the father sadly died two years later."

Ruby nodded thoughtfully. "That would have made her about 2 years old when she came to live with her sister and Robert. Since there were no missing person reports from that time, this leads me back to the one person who fits the mystery and makes sense."

Violet ran down the notes again with her finger before she looked up with a grin. "Our note writer has to be Meredith Denton?"

"Exactly!" Ruby's mind raced with a way to prove it. Evidence that even Nate would find compelling. "Let's send each other our notes so we can collate one file later. From here we should check the land records to see who owned the house on Robert's death. It probably was Agatha and I think that matters when we think of the locked room and who held the key."

"We also need to find out if Nate has done any digging

yet." Violet's eyes twinkled. "Shall we ask him or send Scarlett in to add some pressure?"

Ruby giggled as she put the books together in the middle of the minister's desk. She was elated by how much they had gleaned, even if some of it was still supposition. "I don't think we need to send in the big gun just yet."

They walked down the hall to the main part of the church and found the minister talking to a parishioner in the front row. Except it wasn't any parishioner—it was Alex. Ruby's fiancé lifted his head and his eyes widened at the sight of her. He jumped to his feet and she doubted it was possible to look any guiltier.

"Ruby! I did not know you were here." He shot a pointed glance at the minister.

"Obviously," she teased. "Why are you here?"

"That is between Mr. Turner and me, Ms. Finch," the minister told her dourly.

"Then we'll leave you to your private discussion. Thank you for helping with our research Minister." Ruby marched out of the church with her sister hurrying to keep up.

Once they were outside Violet grabbed her arm. "What was that about?"

"I have no idea," Ruby managed through gritted teeth.

"Really?" Violet responded calmly, while one eyebrow taunted her.

Not knowing what to do with her anguish, but thinking she might explode if she didn't tell her sister, Ruby raised her arms. "I told Alex I wasn't ready to get married just yet and here he is—talking to the minister."

Violet gave a rueful grin. "I hate to break it to you, kiddo, but maybe he was here about something else?"

Ruby chewed her bottom lip. "Do you really think so?"

"Nah." Violet snorted. "He was totally talking to him about marrying you."

Ruby, normally not one for violence, punched her sister in the arm.

"Hey!"

"Hey, yourself. What am I going to do with that man?"

Violet snorted. "Marry him?"

Ruby tried to hit her again, but Violet was too fast.

She backed off with a snicker. "You know you're going to eventually, so I don't know what you're stalling for."

Ruby stamped a foot. "Because everything will change."

Violet smiled gently. "It already has. Baking together can't stop that and neither can prolonging the engagement. It's the way of things and if you love each other then why hold onto something that has already had its day. Things will be different, but that doesn't mean they can't be better."

Ruby's mouth trembled. Violet was the more pragmatic sister and occasionally the glass half empty one. Yet here she was making so much sense that Ruby wanted to blubber like a baby. She was so confused. She loved Alex more than she thought possible, and she wanted a life with him, but she had no experience with living with anyone except her sisters and a college roommate. None of whom were men.

Violet bundled her into her arms. "We are sisters forever, but it really is time for you to move on to the next phase of your life with that wonderful, if annoying man who adores everything about you."

Ruby sniffed into the comforting shoulder as things became clearer. It turned out that all this time, when she had thought she was frightened of change, she was really frightened of being a wife. "What if I don't like marriage?"

"You were made for marriage." Violet huffed. "More

than anyone I know. It's a team sport and you two will make it work."

"How can you be sure?"

"Your organizational skills and your ability to make everyone see your point will ensure complete domination and fealty."

Ruby chuckled.

"Are you okay now?"

Heavy footsteps sounded behind them and Ruby pulled away and wiped at her face as she nodded a second before Alex arrived at her side.

"Ruby, are you crying?"

"Nope. Just had something in my eye," she lied.

"Let me see?"

"It's gone now. What are you doing here?"

"I'm going to head on home," Violet backed away from the tense couple. "See you in the morning, Rubes?"

"Yes, and thanks for helping me, Vi."

Violet smiled encouragingly and hurried down the street.

Ruby looked at her fiancé expectantly.

Alex straightened, though one eye twitched. "I had to discuss a matter with the minister."

"I saw that," she said and waited some more.

He scuffed his shoes on the path. "I asked him, when the time is right, if I could marry in a church."

She blinked in confusion. "What do you mean?"

"I am not from this country." His eyes darted away. "What your church feels about a man like me—I wasn't sure. Maybe I need to do something to make that a possibility."

Ruby put a hand to his cheek. "There is nothing wrong with you, Alex. You are you because of the life you've lived and what you believe, not from where you came from or who your father is. I am proud to marry you, and nobody in a church or elsewhere can stop that from happening, so it doesn't matter what they think or say." She didn't know what the Minister had said, but there was a reason Alex was upset and she meant to get to the bottom of it. "Some people are plain mean and they will never be happy for us, but we don't need their approval."

His mouth worked for a moment or two. "You would marry me anywhere?"

She nodded firmly. "Anywhere."

Alex beamed and dropped to one knee.

"What are you doing?" She giggled. "You've already proposed and I'm pretty sure I said yes."

"I want to make certain it is not a dream. Ruby Finch, will you marry me?"

He looked so solemn that she bit back her laughter and nodded. "I will, Alexander. When?"

He blinked. "Oh. I...as soon as you want."

She tugged his hand so that he stood and then she tucked her arm through his. "Okay. Let's look at some dates on the weekend."

Due to his tough life growing up, Alex didn't shock easily, but her giant of a fiancé had developed big emotions and he was totally taken off guard since he had retaken his freedom. Ruby smiled happily and reached up to kiss his cheek.

"That's exactly how I feel when you try to organize me. Don't worry it will all work out. I promise."

He stiffened just a fraction, then let out a belly laugh. "You are going to keep me on your toes."

Ruby snorted. "You mean on your toes."

He laughed again. "We will see."

Chapter Ten

Having just made the biggest decision of her life; Ruby was oddly calm about it. Violet had managed in her forthright way to take the fear out of the family splitting up and of moving forward. She had done a 'Scarlett' and overthought everything, but now that Ruby saw it for what it was, she would get on with her life and stop thinking of possible negatives. In fact, it already surprised her that she'd let her fears of what might be get to her when she was usually the one who found the good in a situation. Although, the experience also pointed out how similar the sisters were at times, so maybe it wasn't so odd.

They made their way to the diner and Alex cooked her a tasty meal while she did some more online research about the Swansons and he finished work.

Later they sat cuddled on his sofa for a while, making plans for their future. There was so much to discuss, but her stomach was full and being in his arms was so soothing she couldn't focus.

"I would like two children," he said softly.

She tilted her head back so she could gaze up at him. "Not right away, I hope."

"No. When the diner is doing well and you are ready we will decide."

Ruby breathed a sigh of relief. She did want children— just not for a while. "After the wedding, where will we live?"

He hesitated for barely a heartbeat. "Here?"

"Above the diner?" she mused, looking around her at the sparsely furnished room. Alex had been incredibly busy for months and he was particular about what he wanted in his space. His cabin had been much smaller and extremely rustic, so the opportunity to have nice things and be comfortable for once was not lost on him. Plus, as a woodturner he knew quality and it seemed there was little hereabouts to tempt him. The sofa was the one thing he had deemed necessary and she snuggled into him again. It was a very good choice.

She noticed he didn't relax. "Okay, Alex. Tell me what's bugging you now."

He exhaled loudly. "I do not want to be selfish, but I like my privacy and space. This is my first real home and I know it isn't big or pretty. I also know you would prefer to stay with your sisters, but I do not think that would be a good idea once we are married."

Seeing his pain and worry, she sat upright again. "No one said anything about living with Scarlett and Violet."

He shrugged. "You do not want to leave them."

"To be honest I was troubled about moving out," Ruby admitted, "but Violet made me see sense. Our marriage deserves its best chance and we will need a place to get away from our work and families to relax." She waved her hand toward the stairwell. "The thing is, it gets very noisy around the stores and there isn't a yard for children."

He nodded thoughtfully. "Since we do not have children or plans to have them soon, why not live here for a while and save for our own house?"

Ruby chewed her lip for a moment. "I guess that makes sense."

"What makes you hesitate?"

He was good at reading her and she smiled. "There's this house down the road that I think would be perfect for us. George used to live there and it's been empty for quite some time."

Alex frowned. "I heard that George's owner died."

"Yes, but not in the house," she assured him, while omitting that the woman was the previous librarian and that she had been found dead in the library. Alex was not a fan of coincidence.

The lines across his forehead barely relaxed. "That is good. Still, my money is tied up in the diner. I cannot buy you a house yet."

"I've been saving hard, but I guess it wouldn't be enough for a deposit." Ruby winced guiltily at how her comment upset him. His desire to make her happy by giving her everything she wanted was bound to affect him when she voiced plans that he couldn't action. "You know what? It will make buying a house more special after we've saved for it together. Getting married will be more than enough for the time being and your place will do just fine."

He studied her carefully and then kissed the top of her head. "I'm glad you think so."

She did think that, for now, but the house down the road would remain on her wish list. Luckily, dreams were free and if she were honest, most of them had come true thanks to her sisters. When their mom got sick, Scarlett took over the cafe and looking out for the family, including nursing their mom along with Violet. It had been agreed, though Ruby fought it at the time, that she would remain in college and get her degree. If the other two hadn't insisted, she wouldn't have the best job in the world.

There was no other word for it, she was spoilt and better curb her need to have things just so now that she had Alex to consider. Relationships were a lot trickier than she had thought.

"Ruby?"

She was just relaxing again and darn it if there wasn't another tone that meant he wasn't sure how to approach the topic. "Oh dear. What's wrong now?"

There was a lengthy pause. "I saw Nate today."

Her stomach clenched; pretty sure she knew where this was headed. "How is he?"

"He is fine. He told me about your picnic on Sunday."

She let out a long breath. "Did he now?"

"Do not be angry with him. He cares about you and your sisters very much."

"I'm not angry."

He snorted, though his tone reflected that he was not impressed by her deception. "I am glad he told me about this business with the Swansons."

"I'm a librarian. I like old things the same as Violet, and I like puzzles like Scarlett."

"Yes, you all do. The problem is when the three of you get together to solve a puzzle the situation usually becomes dangerous."

She winced. "Well this isn't. We're looking at births and deaths and trying to work out when the author of the letters wrote them, which will tell us when they were alive." She got so excited she didn't notice her slip of tongue. Unfortunately, Alex did.

"There is another letter?" he asked suspiciously.

"Oh. Yes. There are two now. Notes really. On paper ripped from the books." She shrugged. "It's probably someone playing a joke on their friends or family."

"If I could believe that I would be happy. I do not."

Ruby gaped. This was a first. Alex wasn't actually calling her a liar, but it was a thin line. "Why do you feel it isn't the truth?"

He screwed up his nose. "People do not write such awful things as a joke. They write them to scare or to seek help. I think there was no option but to leave the note where you found it. This means that no one could find it unless by accident. Unless it was intended for one person they knew would pick up that book."

She nodded slowly. "You're right. The notes were put in the books, probably at different times."

"If one got no response then another was required."

She nodded again. "The issue with that is if the books were in the library of the house, why would anyone pick up those specific books before any other?"

Alex shrugged as if it were obvious. "The person the note was intended for must like those books."

"Yes! You are so good at this."

He grimaced. "I'm glad if I can help, but all I want is to keep you out of danger."

She squeezed his hand. "I know. Which is why I didn't say anything to you. I don't want you to worry about anything but the diner."

"That cannot happen now that I have met you."

"Ouch. I don't want to be a burden."

He shook his head almost angrily. "You could never be that. I am a better man because of you."

His words touched her so deeply and a warmth crept over her. She kissed his cheek and then made him look her in the eyes. "That is truly lovely to hear, and I am a better woman because of you. The thing is, I do know how good and kind you are. Can you honestly say that if you had found the notes you wouldn't have tried to help this person?"

"They are probably dead," his eyes slipped from hers as he neatly side-stepped the question.

Ruby chewed her bottom lip again. "Probably."

He sighed. "And it makes no difference to you?"

"I'm sorry, it doesn't, because I'll always be thinking what if they are alive and still need help." She wrapped her arms around him and hugged him tight, though her hands didn't meet around his broad back. "I love you Alex, but I must find out the truth."

He sighed again. "I love you too. I will help if I can."

"I know, my love, but you're busy. Please don't trouble yourself."

"It is no trouble if I talk to Swanson when he comes to the diner."

Her heart jumped in her chest. "Wait. Edgar Swanson comes to the diner?"

"Yes. He buys meals and lots of dessert. He says now that he has no cook he is glad that I have opened the diner because he has a sweet tooth. I tell him to make sure he brushes it carefully because of the decay."

She snorted. "And what did he say?"

"He promised he would. What else shall I ask him?"

"Let's just leave him be for a while. At least until I know more about the situation. Okay?"

"Of course. You let me know when and what to say and it will be done. We should always work together."

Ruby knew he was being sincere, but she also recognized that by being involved it gave him the opportunity to keep an eye on her.

Which wasn't such a bad thing.

Chapter Eleven

The next morning, Edgar Swanson swept into the library with a bluster that had nothing to do with weather. His face was a mottled red as he stood at the counter glaring at Ruby.

"What do you think you are doing?" he bellowed.

Bob jumped up from his snooze beneath the desk and growled and George, who had been likewise busy, arched his back and hissed from his spot on the desk.

Edgar backed away, but the anger in his eyes only increased.

"I'm not sure what you mean, Mr. Swanson," Ruby said politely as she smoothed George's fur with one hand and patted Bob on his head.

"Don't give me that innocent look. That same look that made me think you really wanted to see some history. Instead you took advantage of my kind nature and traipsed over my land looking for gossip and scandal."

"I can assure you, that's not what happened," Ruby argued trying hard not to raise her voice.

He slammed his hand on the counter earning another

growl from Bob which he ignored. "That is precisely what happened. I heard afterwards from several sources that you've been delving into my family's history."

Ruby tilted her head, curious as to who those sources might be and came up with a potential name almost immediately. Unable to outright lie, which was a shame because he was a little scary right now, she nodded. "Oh, that. Yes, I am."

"So you admit it!"

"It shouldn't be a surprise that many people are interested in the history of the first ancestors who settled in Cozy Hollow."

He looked confused. "I heard you were after more than that and intended to put my family name into disrepute."

"With history comes many stories and some are worth delving into." Ruby watched him closely as she delivered her next line. "To be honest, it's come to my attention that a woman could have been held at the estate against her will."

"Lies! All lies," he raged again.

"But you do know who I am referring to?" she pressed. "A woman who wanted so desperately to get away that she reached out for help."

He let out a heavy breath. "My Aunt Meredith was touched in the head and, rather than put her into an institution, she was kept safe at home—for her own good. She spoke to anyone who would listen about her situation and of course she put a different slant on things. She couldn't help herself."

Ruby heard his anguish and something more. He loved his aunt. "Thank you for telling me. That clears things up nicely."

He eyed her skeptically. "Are you saying that's all you wanted to know? That your investigating is done?"

Ruby screwed up her nose. "Since you ask. There were no dates of birth for the babies in the graveyard and no last name. Could you shed some light on them?"

"It's no one's business who they were." His voice rose and his hands gripped the counter, knuckles white.

She got the impression that he regretted coming to see her and possibly being so frank. However, this might be her only chance to get more information from him, so she felt the need to press. "Why is it such an issue who they were after all these years? Times change and babies born out of wedlock aren't such a stigma these days."

He stiffened. "You may find it a usual occurrence in your circles, but I can assure you it is still frowned upon in mine."

"I understand, and I'm not trying to embarrass you or your family. As a librarian, I just think it's important to keep accurate records. Any records of the babies, which were probably twins due to the same date of death, are missing." Ruby took a deep breath. "As is the final resting place of your Aunt Meredith."

His face reddened again and he blinked rapidly. "She was buried in Portland."

While Ruby noted that he didn't deny the babies were twins, she tutted at the obvious fabrication. "And yet, there are no records to prove that."

Edgar reared back. "Are you calling me a liar?"

"Not at all." Ruby swallowed hard, appreciating that she was alone with a man she didn't know. A man who was getting angrier by the minute. "I know that records can get messed up, Mr. Swanson. I'd just like confirmation of where she was buried and if the twins were hers."

"And I would like you to mind your own business and let the dead rest in peace," he growled. "Is it so hard for you and your sisters to keep your noses out of other people's affairs?"

Bob rumbled deeper and Ruby put a hand on his collar.

"I'm sure it's hard having no living relatives to share your family's history with," she said gently.

Edgar blinked, but much slower this time. "What does that have to do with anything?"

She clasped her hands together, experiencing some guilt at pushing the man to talk of things that he clearly found abhorrent. "It's obvious that you feel an obligation to keep the family secrets and I appreciate that. The Finch family have had their share of them, but since you seem to be the last of the Swansons, I want to point out that there is no one left to care about those secrets except to ensure that they never harmed anyone."

He wiped his face with both hands. Hands that shook. "It may have slipped your notice that I am very much alive. I care. I've always cared even when no one else did."

Ruby didn't think she had ever met a more wretched man. Filled with sadness and anger, from what she could gather, he was alone in the world except for some distant cousins. Maybe there were other reasons for this. Reasons why he had no wife or children. Or even a friend. But her heart could not help being touched, despite his anger being directed at her.

"Mr. Swanson, you can let all this go now and live your life any way you choose. What your ancestors did has no bearing on you," she told him gently.

He paled. "You haven't a clue what you're talking about."

"Probably not," she admitted. "Look, I'm truly sorry if this is dragging up bad memories. None of us can walk in another's shoes, but you were a young man when your aunt lost her babies. Whatever happened to her was not your fault."

Edgar shuddered and Ruby saw that she had not just hit a nerve. He was reliving some hellish moment and she would bet a baguette that he knew exactly what happened back then—and it wasn't good.

Of course, Ruby was certain from the outset of this mystery that things had not ended well for the person who wrote the notes. However, she had hoped to be wrong, and now the reasons why the woman got locked away raced around in her mind. Was it really over mental health issues, which were treated with more humanity these days, or was it due to the pregnancy? That line in the note about being an embarrassment nagged at her.

Edgar was also lost in thought and while she waited for him to return to her, she studied the man who knew more than he wanted to share. The way the lines in his face pulled at his jowls suggested he was not much of a smiler. Instead he had deep grooves along his forehead, which seemed permanent.

It took a few moments before his eyes eventually met hers. He was impossibly paler now, though his voice was steadier. "As I said. You don't know what you are talking about. For your own sake, you should leave things be."

Ruby's eyes widened. "Are you threatening me, Mr. Swanson?"

Edgar glanced down at the dog who was making a low continuous rumble and took a step back. "That is not my style. Take it for the warning it is and don't go looking for the trouble that will surely follow if you dig into a past that should stay buried." He turned and left without a goodbye.

Ruby let out a shuddering breath. Was he the type to harm a person? She really wasn't sure. He had a temper, but didn't everyone when provoked? After all, she had challenged his way of thinking and the way his family had dealt with a difficult situation.

"Anyone would be upset by that, right?" she said aloud.

Bob whined and George sauntered to the door. Ruby followed and let him out. Edgar had disappeared, yet the cat hurried purposefully around the corner of the library. Part of her hoped he was going to follow Edgar and see where he went. He wouldn't likely report back to her like some spy, although stranger things had happened.

Ruby sighed. The urge to tag along was strong, but she couldn't shut the library on a whim.

Chapter Twelve

The day had been busy and when Nate came through the open back door of the Finch's cottage after a quick cursory knock, his face a picture of annoyance apparently directed at one sister in particular, Ruby sighed and her hands stilled over the potatoes she was peeling at the sink. "Hi, Nate."

"What are you up to now?" he growled.

She glanced at the potatoes then raised an eyebrow. "I assume you don't mean right this minute. Can you give me a hint?"

His nostrils flared. "You know what I mean. You've upset Edgar Swanson and he's laid a complaint."

"Don't tell me you're taking it seriously?" Scarlett asked from where she folded washing at the kitchen table.

"I take all complaints seriously," he assured her tartly.

"Let me rephrase that," she said just as tartly. "Ruby has been asking questions about a woman who can't ask them for herself. She is not harassing anyone when the person in question attacked her at her place of work. If they don't wish to talk to her, then fine, but they can't stop her from looking up records that are public knowledge."

The bluster slipped from him like a deflated balloon. "I don't understand why you want to carry this note business any further."

"Call it intuition or a feeling, but there is more to this than Edgar Swanson is willing to share." Ruby tilted her head. "Aren't you even slightly curious as to what happened to his aunt?"

His mouth pursed. "There have been a spate of burglaries and people who are alive are upset about that. Forgive me if I think my time is better spent looking into crimes that are current and therefore more urgent."

"So all crimes that are more than a few days old are considered non-urgent?"

"It's dependent on the crime," he admitted.

"See, that's the point. If we don't know why, how, or when Meredith died, then the urgency has probably been overlooked. Maybe it won't matter to her if we find her captor or killer, but what if the culprit is wandering around our town?"

"You've built this into one of your stories. Edgar gave you an explanation..."

"Since he lied, that explanation has no foundation. There is no proof that a) Meredith died, b) what she died of, or c) where she's buried."

He ran a hand through his hair and was about to speak when Alex appeared behind him.

Ruby rushed to his side. "What are you doing here? Is the diner okay?"

He nodded briskly. "I heard you are in trouble."

Ruby rounded on Nate. "You spoke to Alex about me?"

Nate blanched under her gaze and he twisted the brim of his hat in his hand. "I mentioned your chat with Edgar."

Her foot tapped on the wooden floor. "Why would you do that?"

"So he could talk some sense into you."

Ruby felt her blood pressure rise, but she didn't have to say a word.

A long slim finger waved in Nate's face. "You may be the sheriff, but you are also our friend. If Ruby says there is something to all this business, then we believe her. If you don't, then you are entitled to your opinion, but you don't get to gang up on any of us."

His eyes widened and Ruby noticed he edged back a few inches. Scarlett was a force to be reckoned with and though he watched her sister warily, Alex stepped forward.

"Nate is my friend too. He was concerned and I appreciate that he told me. How could he keep his worry to himself when he knows of my feelings for Ruby? Cozy Hollow is a small town. We will always hear about your exploits," Alex told her, calmer now.

Ruby sighed and looked to her sisters. Violet shrugged, her eyes twinkling. Scarlett raised an eyebrow that said it was Ruby's call how things went from here.

"Fine. You were both concerned, which is sweet," Ruby began. "I can't stop that, but you are not going to be helicopter boyfriends or fiancés. We don't want or need it."

"Here, here," said Violet.

"Maybe you don't want it, but you have needed our help in the past," Nate reminded them all.

While Ruby couldn't deny his statement, she didn't have to like it.

Suddenly Nate changed tack. "Can't you just leave it for a while? Just until I can give it more time."

Ruby glanced at her sisters again. The last thing she wanted was to cause a rift between Scarlett and Nate and she certainly didn't want Alex to be worried about her every minute. "If time is what you need before you can help us, then I agree to stay away from Edgar Swanson, but don't expect me to keep off the internet."

He gave a small bow. "I wouldn't dream of it and I'm sorry if I upset you all by barging in here tonight. I am the sheriff, but I'm also your friend and that makes things a little more personal."

"I know and we're all good." Ruby let him off the hook, not because she thought he would act differently next time, but because he really did care. She just hoped that he'd eventually understand that the sisters had to follow their instincts as well as their hearts. It would certainly help his relationship with Scarlett.

"Good. I'm glad this is resolved." Alex looked at his watch and frowned. "We should go to the diner for pumpkin pie and ice cream. It is from your recipe, Scarlett, and I would like your opinion if it is good enough. Plus, I have left Lexie to look after the place, so I better hurry before she tries to cook something."

The others laughed which lightened the mood considerably. Lexie couldn't cook worth a darn and everyone knew it. The women piled into Ruby's car and followed the men to town. It wasn't far and soon they were sitting in a booth at the diner.

Lexie nervously handed them menus. The sisters were confused, until they saw a familiar face at the kitchen serving window plating a toasted sandwich.

A rumble from Nate caused Scarlett to jump to her feet. She hurried to the window to circumvent any showdown. "Hey, Sam. How are you?"

His eyes ranged over the group worriedly resting on Nate. "Good thanks, Scarlett. How are you?"

"Really great. The café is doing well now and my sisters are behaving themselves. As much as they can."

Ruby laughed, but not in the usual bubbly way she was known for. Scarlett and Sam were once an item and would have gotten married. Only, it transpired that Sam was and had always been in love with Lexie. He'd given up hope that they would ever be together and so Scarlett had become his second choice. With the murder of Lexie's fiancé (an arranged marriage) things changed rapidly and it was clear where Sam's allegiance and love lay. Scarlett had been hurt at first, until she realized that she too was settling. The flirtation between her and Nate was quick to reignite and Sam was mostly forgotten.

Unfortunately, Nate had not forgiven Sam for hurting Scarlett and he was looking daggers at the paramedic, who had once been his friend. "What are you doing in there?" he asked loudly.

Sam winced. "I came to give Lexie a ride home when her shift is finished and she said she was hungry, so I made her a sandwich. I hope that's okay, Alex."

Alex's eyes never left Nate's face. "Whatever my sister wants she should have."

Nate stared back at him for a moment, perhaps sensing whatever he said next would be out of line. "I suddenly have no appetite. I'll trust you to see them home." He nodded at the sisters.

"Of course," Alex said matter-of-factly.

Ruby saw his relief at Nate's decision. Though Alex was indeed Nate's friend, Lexie's happiness was very important to him and she had chosen Sam. Nate had to get over it and accept that Sam wasn't going anywhere, or there would always be this tension between the group. She understood both sides, but it was very awkward.

"I have an early start tomorrow," Scarlett called across the room. "Could I get a ride, Nate?"

His expression softened and he held the door open for her.

"Well, that was—a lot," Lexie muttered when it closed behind them.

"He'll come around," Ruby told them assuredly. "He just needs a bit more time."

"I suspect there's not ever going to be enough time," Sam said sadly.

While Alex sliced pie, Ruby sighed deeply. Nate and Sam had been such good friends before the drama. It was such a shame that Nate couldn't let it go when the four people involved had what they wanted. They were so lucky —Nate just didn't seem to realize it.

Unlike Edgar. The thought popped unbidden into her mind. What did that man want? To keep his family's secret of babies born out of wedlock? But what if there was another secret? She simply knew he was hiding something.

Chapter Thirteen

The kitchen hummed with machines. Scarlett pushed back her hair with a forearm. "I can't tell you how glad I am that you two are here this morning. With the knitting group having an early breakfast meeting so that Aunt Olivia and Gail Norman can attend, I would have been short-staffed."

Ruby smiled at her. "It's good we can make a difference as well as spend time together." She enjoyed their early morning baking sessions even more than she had imagined and was convinced the three of them were closer than ever, even though Violet liked to have a moan about the sleep she was missing out on.

As if to prove her point, Violet snorted.

"I'd already heard about the meeting from Gail. She is so in love with the craft store, she hasn't been making time for a catch up with the knitting group and Leona's having hissy fits left and right about fair weather friends—whatever that means."

Scarlett tutted. "You know Leona wanted to buy into the store with Gail instead of you and Phin. The trouble started when she decided to take over and force her ideas onto Gail. Then you sided with Gail over her."

"I challenge you to say you wouldn't have done the same thing. Can you imagine working with Leona in any capacity?"

"Please don't talk to me about Leona." Ruby huffed. "She was in the diner for lunch on Monday and was so rude to Lexie and Alex I wanted to ask her to leave."

Scarlett gave a mock gasp. "You were that angry with her?"

"It's no joke. She hadn't tried one thing and was already making little digs about the ethnicity of each item on the menu while comparing it to 'proper' food."

"Did she like it once she'd tasted it?"

"She ate every scrap off her plate, so I'm guessing she did," Ruby huffed again. "Then she told Lexie that it wasn't the worst food she'd ever eaten."

"Lucky Alex for getting such a glowing review." Violet rolled her eyes. "Leona's been having a dig at Gail too. Ever since I thwarted her investing money into the store, her jealousy has leveled up and now she can't say a good word about the place—or Gail."

Ruby sighed. "Poor Gail."

"Poor Gail indeed. The day we finished setting up the store, Leona stopped by to offer an unasked-for critique. All she did was pick fault with everything. Gail was in tears by the time Leona left. I wish I could say it had gotten better. However, I do believe that Gail is becoming a little more immune to the barbs and staying out of Leona's way is a big part of that."

Ruby took berry muffins from a pan and automatically placed them on a rectangular tray as she recalled the thoughtful way Leona had looked at her in the diner.

"Leona has far too much time on her hands and with Linda spending more time at the store with Gail, I guess she's lonely."

"I wondered how long it would be before you found a feasible reason for her behavior," Violet chuckled.

"What do you mean?"

"You always want to find a person's good points. Even after they've behaved badly."

Ruby shrugged. "We all behave badly from time to time."

"Agreed, but not on such a regular basis." Violet groaned. "I'd like to see Leona have more compassion occasionally, so I don't think badly of her every darn day."

Ruby chewed her bottom lip as she mixed a batch of frosting for a chocolate cake. "She has done some good for the community and has always supported the café with her custom."

"Granted, but it doesn't give her license to rain on everyone's parade to make herself feel better."

Ruby silently agreed, but she had occasionally seen Leona's wistfulness when she thought no one was looking. She didn't believe for one minute that making digs at her friends made Leona feel better. At least, not for any length of time. The woman couldn't seem to help herself.

The bell above the shop door chimed and pulled her from her reverie. Scarlett wiped her hands on a towel before going out front and Ruby followed with the tray of muffins.

"Good morning," Gail called. "I hope we're not too early."

From behind her, Linda gave an appreciative sniff at the air and a cheery wave.

"Not at all," Scarlett said as she waited for them to get

settled at the table by the window. "What will it be this morning?"

"We'll order our food once Leona gets here, but I'll have a cappuccino please."

"Me too," Linda echoed, looking decidedly nervous when the door opened again.

"Goodness, there's a nip in the air this morning." Aunt Olivia bustled inside and removed her coat. "Thankfully, it's lovely and warm in here." She smiled at her nieces before turning to her friends. "No Leona yet?"

"Perhaps she's ill?" Linda said almost hopefully.

"I doubt it." Olivia sent Ruby and Scarlett a wink. "She's made of tough stuff and besides, illness wouldn't dare tackle her."

The other women snickered just as the door opened, wiping the smile off their faces. This was the first time since Gail had bought into Violet's shop that the four of them had been together.

"Leona!" Linda yelped.

"Don't act so surprised." Leona's voice was disdainful. "I organized the meeting, if you recall."

Linda seemed to shrink in her chair and Ruby noted there was no sign of their knitting paraphernalia, which could mean that none had the intention of having a leisurely breakfast. It was a little sad. The group had been meeting here for years and to lose the closeness they once had over petty jealousy didn't seem right.

Ruby truly wanted everyone to be happy. As happy as she was currently might be a tall order, with the whole marrying such a wonderful man thing. Certainly not being anything close to miserable would be nice. Miserable like Leona—and Edgar Swanson. She almost dropped the tray as she slid it into the display case.

Edgar was preying on her mind as was Meredith. She didn't know why exactly, but the strong feeling that there was so much more to the story couldn't be ignored. Cozy Hollow was such a small town that someone other than the family had to know more details.

As she stood, her eyes met Leona's. Ruby smiled and Leona looked away. That was odd. Sure, Leona was in a bad mood lately, but she had never been outright rude to Ruby before. Wheels whirred in her head. Leona was the oldest of the group. No one knew exactly how old since the woman was incredibly private, but Ruby had heard the women talk about being at school together. That could make the whole group close to Edgar Swanson's age.

"You're staring," Violet nudged her and Ruby almost fell into the display case.

Ruby grabbed her sister's hand and pulled her into the kitchen. "I have a hunch Leona could have information about the Swansons and I think we should persuade her to share it."

Chapter Fourteen

"Good luck with that." Violet snorted and tugged her hand free. "Anyway, how did you come to that conclusion when as far as I know you haven't spoken to her about any of this?"

"Leona just snubbed me."

"Oh, poor Ruby." Violet snorted again. "I promise, it won't kill you if the odd person doesn't find you perfect."

Ruby sniffed, knowing she would never change Violet's perception that she needed to be liked. To be fair, she wasn't entirely wrong, Ruby admitted to herself. "Whatever. I'm serious, Vi."

"I figured you were, but you can't point fingers when you have no proof. And you can't ask questions of the customers which you know are likely to upset them. Scarlett would throw a fit."

Ruby chewed her bottom lip. "I see your point."

Violet gasped in mock horror. "Now, you're scaring me."

"As if you're scared of anything. Besides, we do agree on some things."

"Yes, but usually after you've coerced us into seeing your way is the best."

Ruby rolled her eyes. "Stop exaggerating."

With a shrug, Violet removed her apron. "You can stay here and get yourself into trouble without my help. I have a store to run."

Ruby glanced at the clock and removed hers too. "I didn't realize the time. I need to check on Alex before I open the library."

"I hear the place is doing great."

"It's doing okay, but not great." Ruby explained. "We need to advertise more and get people from nearby towns to come try the diner. More importantly, people who aren't so set in their ways."

"Do you think people from Good Fortune and Maple Falls would come this far?"

"It's only twenty or thirty minutes to them so I don't see why not." Ruby sighed wistfully. "Just imagine if we could get people from a large town like Destiny."

Violet snapped her fingers. "Since he can't afford a lot of advertising, why don't you get some more of the posters made that you put up around town. Then I can take them with me and pin them up in other places that I source antiques from."

"What a great idea, Vi. People with treasures from exotic places would surely love to try new cuisine."

"I wouldn't get my hopes too high if I was you. Often they're selling those treasures because they have no choice."

Ruby's excitement waned a little. "Oh, I hadn't considered why they would part with precious items. That's so sad."

Violet nodded. "It is hard sometimes to offer a fair price

when I know there won't be much in it for me if I do. It kind of defeats the purpose of being in business."

Ruby kissed her cheek. "You can try to be all staunch and grumpy, but I know the real Violet."

Violet glared as best she could, but Ruby simply laughed at her and together they went back into the café to say goodbye to Scarlett, who had just finished taking orders.

"Leaving the ship?" she teased quietly.

Ruby looked over Scarlett's shoulder at the knitting group who did not appear to be enjoying each other's company. "Will you be okay if Olivia is tied up with her meeting and can't help?"

"It won't be a problem because they didn't order breakfasts. Muffins and coffee all round today."

"I can understand Olivia not needing a breakfast when she can have whatever she wants here, but I thought it was a breakfast meeting," Ruby protested.

"Me too." Scarlett rolled her eyes then laughed. "Never mind. It makes things easier and means Olivia will be on board by the time the next rush hits. Thanks for your help this morning and have a great day."

Ruby and Violet gave Olivia a wave as they left and Gail and Linda waved back as well, while Leona's eyes narrowed and she looked away again.

"Ohhh. I see what you mean," Violet whispered when they got back to the kitchen. "You are not her favorite person today at all."

"So, I wasn't imagining it." Ruby grabbed her bag and held the back door open for Violet.

"Nope. Though I do think I was included in that look. She must have heard about our visit to the minister."

Ruby stopped in the middle of the path. "Why do you say that?"

"She does the flowers for the church and she's uber nosey. I hear the minister can be a bit of a gossip too."

"He was hardly in a gossiping mood when we were there," Ruby mused.

"Didn't you know?" Violet put on a tart voice. "He dislikes the young people."

Ruby chuckled. "We're the young people?"

"In his book, apparently anyone under forty is young. How old do you think he is?"

"Past retirement age for sure. Maybe close to seventy. I heard they had a young minister visit with a view to taking over the parish, but the minister wasn't open to it and apparently, made the poor man's life very difficult."

"I don't remember that."

"It was when you were off with Phin studying to be an assessor and it wasn't the first time they tried to get him to retire properly. By the way, I've been meaning to ask, are you still happy to stay in Cozy Hollow?"

Violet smiled broadly. "I am the happiest I've ever been, Rubes."

Ruby couldn't help the happy sigh and she wrapped her arm through her sister's. "It shows."

Violet nodded. "It's like a spring uncoiled inside me. Even Gail with her fussing can't mess with that too much."

"I'm so pleased that you finally found your place in the world and I think having the craft store and antiques together was a stroke of genius."

"Me too," Violet agreed. "On both counts."

They laughed all the way down the street where Violet left her at the door of the store and Ruby continued to the diner. She only had a few minutes, but she had to see Alex. She went to the back door and let herself in.

Alex was loading an industrial slow cooker with lumps

of pork belly. He looked over his arm and grinned. "Good morning, fiancée."

"Good morning, husband-to-be."

He dropped the lid, pressed a couple of buttons, and then washed his hands. She waited patiently and was rewarded with a bear hug, dialed down so he didn't hurt her, yet it still lifted her off her feet. Then he kissed her and she could have been flying.

"Wow," she whispered into his neck.

"I think it was more than wow."

She nodded and rubbed her cheek against his. "Now that I know you are good, I better get to the library."

"I wish you could stay longer."

"Me too, but my customers won't be happy if they can't get in. I have a school class coming from the beach this morning."

The Carver Corporation had created a small town for its employees. Even smaller than Cozy Hollow, it had a couple of mixed aged classes and a tiny room that they called a library. Ruby donated extra books when she had them but encouraged the principal and teachers to come to the Cozy Hollow library on a regular basis for a wider range. Plus, she loved seeing the children.

"That will be fun." Alex grinned, reading her expression, if not her mind.

"It always is. They're so eager to learn that it makes me tingle with happiness."

"I think this tingle is catching."

She laughed and gave him a quick peck on the lips before hurrying out the door in case she said something silly. When he looked at her the way he did, she could barely breathe and despite not wanting to rush into a family, the thought of having children with Alex was often in her mind these days.

Naturally, that made her think of poor Meredith and the twins that never, or barely, lived. While it wasn't confirmed, Edgar hadn't denied that the babies buried on the estate were twins, despite her mentioning it twice. How tragic would that be to carry a life—two lives—and lose them? Ruby shook her head and forced herself to think about the next few hours, when there would be an abundance of laughter, questions, and if she were lucky a hug or two. These children could be reserved, but once they warmed up they were just like any others and loved attention and praise.

Ruby knew she was a lucky woman because she got to witness and encourage their excitement in learning new things.

Chapter Fifteen

The whole school was here today, including the new principal. Jerome Granger had arrived at the Harmony Beach school a few months ago bringing a refreshing take on learning that the retiring principal hadn't been interested in. Jerome agreed with Ruby that every child deserved a chance to broaden their knowledge and experience new things. Since the pupils in his school had not been given this opportunity, Jerome was on a mission to right that.

After all the drama with the murder of Lexie's husband and the outing of Alex as the love child of her father, the Carver Corporation had lost a lot of its hold over the town. When the principal retired, the community looked for new blood who had no ties or history to the Carver family. Jerome was the result and Ruby couldn't have chosen a better man for the job.

They sat drinking coffee at her desk while the children had some quiet time reading. The accompanying teachers spoke quietly at a table near the window overlooking Main Street.

"You're miles away," Jerome whispered.

Ruby blinked. "Sorry. I have a lot on my mind these days."

"More than usual?" he teased.

She nodded. "Yes. So much more."

"I'd have thought that a wedding to arrange as well as your fiancé's new restaurant opening was plenty."

"You would think so," she laughed. "It turns out, I have a terrible habit of worrying about other people and trying to fix things."

"Hah. I don't doubt that for a minute. Watching you with these kids, it's easy to see that you want to give them the best experience each time they come here and I'm sure all your patrons get the same treatment."

"That's what I hope for. I would have been lost without books, and if they can help another child find their passion, then I'll do everything I can to aid that."

"I couldn't have said it better." He smiled wryly. "Although, learning can be a blessing or a curse when you don't know when to stop."

This comment surprised her. "I never thought of it like that."

"That's because you found your path."

"And you haven't?"

"I have now. Why I never considered being a principal I'll never know. I thought I had to learn about everything otherwise I was a failure. It's weird to admit it now, but I was never happy just being a teacher."

Ruby shrugged. "You were searching for the thing that made it all worthwhile."

"Yes, that's it exactly."

They grinned at each other recognizing a kindred spirit.

"Alright, tell me what you're worried about. Only if you really want to hear, and only if your fiancé wouldn't kill me over it."

She snorted. "He can be a little possessive, but Alex is a gentle giant—unless provoked."

His eyes twinkled. "Yeah, let's not provoke him."

"Okay. He does know about this, and it is sensitive, but I don't think he'd mind me telling you."

"Now I'm intrigued."

Ruby took a deep breath and told him of the books, notes, graveyard, the twins, and Meredith.

Jerome ruffled his dark curls with both hands. "What a story."

"It's fascinating, but not complete is it?"

"Not by a long way." He tilted his head. "Have you considered who the father might be?"

"Many times, and I have written a list of possibilities, but Violet and I couldn't confirm any connections. The Swansons were/are a very private family and there was no mention of any marriages or any deaths around that time."

Jerome looked startled, then leaned forward. "The Swansons, you say? That is interesting. I hear they were old money."

Pleased he was so interested, she nodded. "The family has been in the house since it was built. They were proud of their achievements, according to articles I've managed to uncover. Then it seems that everything stagnated when the patriarch passed away."

"You mean when Edgar Swanson took over and the place went into a decline?" he asked dryly.

She blinked. "Do you know the family?"

"What? Oh, no, not really."

Ruby found his reply odd. Or was it the careful way he said he didn't really know them? She continued, keeping a watch on his reaction. "The decline wasn't totally Edgar's fault, because as far as I can tell he wasn't in charge. Apparently, his mother ran the farm until she recently passed away."

"Well that sheds a new light on things." Jerome's face cleared a little. "Although, they must have known they were in difficulties long before it got to the stage of selling. Surely they could have done something to keep the place going?"

"Since I don't have access to the financial records, that's not clear to me," Ruby admitted. "But I've seen the place now and it didn't get to that state in just a couple of years. You can tell Edgar's angry about his situation which is understandable. Losing the family home must rankle."

"Probably, although like I said, you'd think he could have done something to avoid having to sell."

"Maybe but imagine having to be the one that had to make that decision. He's a very proud man and I think us snooping around the place was the last straw. We didn't handle it well which was my fault. In hindsight I should have waited until the house was in the hands of the new owner." Ruby hadn't let herself dwell on this too much, but it was a relief to finally admit it, even if it was to Jerome and not her sisters.

Jerome clasped his hands together around one knee. "It is a shame, but not the end of the world. I might be able to help you with your search for answers."

Ruby wasn't sure where this was going, but Jerome had an intriguing twinkle in his eyes. "I'd be grateful for any help, but how could you do that?"

"Are you free tonight after work?"

She shifted awkwardly in her seat. "I guess so. What did you have in mind?"

He roared with laughter, earning him a tut or two from one of the older teachers. "Sorry," he whispered to her before turning back to Ruby. "I have met Alex several times and I can assure you, attractive as you are, I am not hitting on you."

Ruby let out a long breath and giggled. The last thing she wanted was to lose his friendship over a silly misunderstanding. "Well, you did have me worried for a second or two. What are you proposing?"

He snorted and hid it with a cough. "Here's your first answer. The Swansons' place? I bought it."

"No!"

"Shhh!"

"Sorry." She winced at the teacher who was old-school and did not approve of the youngish principal, let alone ferrying the whole school around the countryside to learn. Ruby leaned closer to Jerome and lowered her voice. "I know it was run down, but that place would have cost a lot of money to purchase." She put a hand to her mouth guiltily. "Sorry that was rude. It's none of my business what you buy and how much it cost."

He put a hand up. "Let's not pretend you don't want to know why I bought it. First let me just say, the place wasn't as expensive as you might think given its size. Secondly, you obviously only saw the outside. Trust me, the inside is much, much worse."

Ruby thought her head might explode. "This is wonderful news. Not the fact that it's worse, but that you can show me around. That is what you mean to do by telling me all this, isn't it?" she asked hopefully.

Jerome grinned. "Absolutely. I've kind of impressed

myself at negotiating the sale and it will be nice to have a sympathetic face see it and perhaps not tell me what an idiot I am for buying such a dud."

She restrained herself from clapping her hands. "Can Violet and Scarlett come?"

"Need a chaperone?" he teased.

"No, but if I didn't invite them, they would not be happy. Violet especially would be furious."

"The more the merrier." He grinned. "Plus, I'd like Violet's take on a few of the pieces I bought off Edgar."

"She'll love that."

He nodded as he stood, then stretched. "Good. What about tonight? Shall I meet you all there?"

Ruby grinned. "Tonight would be perfect. And yes, since we'll be coming from different directions, meeting you there is best. Will 6 p.m. be okay?"

"Perfect." He checked his watch and clapped his hands. The children obediently closed their books and stood. They lined up in an orderly fashion for Ruby to stamp the books they wanted to borrow. Most had two or three and some had more. She turned a blind eye to the two-book policy, made in her predecessors' times due to the library not being huge. These kids deserved the opportunity to have as much chance to read as possible. As far as Ruby was concerned, rules could be changed and should fit the circumstances.

Half an hour later they were gone and silence reigned once more. Except for Bob's snores. He was always exhausted after the children's visit. They loved him and he had as many pats in two hours as he might in a week when they came to town.

George slunk out from under Ruby's desk. While enjoying some attention, he found the children to be too much and hid when they arrived.

Before she cleaned up, Ruby messaged Violet to come see her at lunchtime if she could. She didn't tell her why, ensuring a piqued interest. Plus, she wanted to see Violet's face when she told her sister about the potential treasures that Jerome had purchased.

Chapter Sixteen

Ruby pulled up the estate details on the internet. It was built in the late 1800's and had been in the Swanson family until now. These details she already knew.

Jerome was only the second owner and she imagined he would look after the building as best he could, but it would take a lot of money to get it to a decent livable state. He was a principal, so she couldn't see how he was going to manage that on his salary. Last year when things had been especially tough, the town had organized a working bee at the Finch family home. It had been embarrassing and wonderful in equal measure, but they couldn't have done so many renovations without help.

The principal was new to the area, and many people in Cozy Hollow wouldn't know him at all. Sadly, she doubted if a working bee for him would get enough people willing to help. Suddenly Ruby remembered that Jerome hadn't said why he had bought the place. It was far too big for one person and even if he was thinking of starting a family, they would still only need a fraction of that space.

She shook her head which was full of questions she should probably keep to herself. Jerome had confided in her and even if it would be common knowledge soon, given the nature of a small town and gossip, for now he deserved the chance to decide when to tell other people.

The library door opening jarred her from her thoughts. Leona entered purposefully and Ruby pasted on a bright smile.

"Good morning, Mrs. Wolf."

"Ruby," she nodded. "I've been thinking a great deal about this business with the Swansons."

"Really?" Surprised didn't scratch the surface of how this announcement affected Ruby, but she was certainly interested in what Leona had to say. "And what did you decide?"

"I must admit that at first I was very annoyed that you and your sisters were meddling in other people's lives and I was set to tell you to mind your own business."

"I'm sorry you feel that way, but..."

Leona put a hand up. "I'm not finished. Violet can be very annoying, and disrespectful, but I have always considered you the most practical of your sisters."

Ruby gaped. So Leona hadn't been angry with her, but with Violet?

"Close your mouth dear," Leona continued. "Anyway, I have thought about things long and hard and decided that I will trust you for now, even though I have no doubts you will tell your sister everything we discuss. I'm here to ask if you are still looking for Meredith Denton?"

"Yes," Ruby managed, while reeling from the shock of Leona's admissions. "Do you know something?"

"I've lived in this town all my life. I know a lot of things."

Ruby couldn't argue with that, and forced herself to wait patiently for the difficult woman to explain what that could mean and wasn't disappointed.

"When I considered what you said about no one knowing where she was, I admit that my conscience was pricked. I went to school with Meredith. She was a bit older, but not at all academic. In fact, she was held back twice."

"Did she have learning issues?"

Leona's eyebrows joined at the interruption and Ruby bit her lip, still musing over the woman having a conscience, but not wanting to alienate or stop her from saying more. She had to wait a heartbeat or two before Leona decided to continue.

"Meredith preferred reading novels above any school-work and was caught more than once with a one of them inside a textbook. Her sister was not impressed and when she did attend, Meredith wasn't allowed to visit with us outside of school. After she left, I never saw her at anything until she joined the church choir a year or so later. We were both members and we chatted between songs as well as before and after practice. She did not discuss her home life, but it was clear she was unhappy with the restrictions placed on her by her sister. Edgar would sit on a pew at the back of the church reading until it was time to take her home so there was no chance of extending the time in town."

There was a lengthy pause as if she expected the next question to be important. What did Leona know that she wanted Ruby to extract from her and why wasn't she willingly offering the information if it was so important?

"What was Meredith like?"

Leona's eyes widened. "She was beautiful, kind, and— desperate."

Ruby blinked. "How so?"

"She was lonely. With only Edgar, a few years younger, for company, you can imagine that once she left school conversation with other people her age was rare. Anyone who encountered her, and I mean the people who worked there or dropped supplies to the farm, would say the same thing. Poor Meredith was starved of friends her own age. Wherever I saw her, she always hovered on the edge of a group of people, waiting to join into a conversation, but incapable of beginning one. I thought she had something wrong with her, some insecurity of not being intelligent enough, but then I wondered if it was this desperation that made it seem so."

Clearly it troubled Leona to say these words and she seemed reluctant to continue. Had she also lost a friend when Meredith disappeared?

"Did you notice if she was close to anyone around the farm, or hear of a friendship outside of the choir?"

"There was no one that I know of. Except for the minister who took a shine to her and spent more time with Meredith than the rest of us. I think he felt sorry for her as I did."

Ruby nodded slowly. "What was her relationship with Edgar like?"

"Though she was a few years older, Meredith deferred to him. When he said it was time to go, they left."

"Would you say she liked Edgar, or was scared of him?"

Leona snorted. "She certainly wasn't scared. Meredith adored him, and he adored her. They were closer than if they had been brother and sister and it would have been right if they were. His mother might have ordered him to act as a chaperone, but he didn't seem to find the task onerous. It appeared to me that he felt a responsibility to her, and her happiness. Considering her lack of time spent away from the estate, he was undoubtedly her buffer."

"Was he always kind to Meredith?"

"Yes." Leona sounded wistful and gave a small smile. "Edgar made sure she put her hat and coat on when they left a place and he held them for her while we practiced. He waited patiently while she chatted with the minister or one of the other girls and he never nagged her to hurry. Often he had a treat for her for the walk home."

"It doesn't sound like a relationship that engendered fear," Ruby mused.

"Not at all. The worst thing I can say about Meredith is though she was a beautiful girl, she couldn't sing a note that didn't bend your ear in a bad way. No one wanted to stand near her and it was just as well that the minister offered her extra lessons. I fear she would have been kicked out if not for that."

"That was kind of him. Did Edgar stay for these lessons?"

"As far as I know, he did. I don't think he would have left Meredith in town and certainly she would not have been allowed to walk home by herself. They were a very proper family."

"Growing up, did you see much of Edgar?"

"Not a great deal. Our time together was minimal. He would come by to collect Meredith from her class while she was at school and was friendly enough, but my understanding was that he had a lot of work waiting for him at the estate. When Meredith was taken out of school, he simply went straight home at the end of the day. There was no hanging around the playground or going to the diner with any of us."

"You keep saying Meredith was taken out of school? Did she not complete her education?"

Leona shook her head. "Sadly Meredith wasn't very academic and my mother told me that she was going to be home-schooled. I assumed the late Mrs. Swanson thought she might fare better with one-on-one attention."

Ruby nodded thoughtfully. "Thank you for telling me all this. May I ask why you decided I should know?"

Leona pursed her lips. "I hear that the sheriff isn't keen on looking into this. Meredith was a sweet girl and if I can help find out what happened to her, then I should."

Ruby smiled at the often-acerbic woman. "I feel that way too."

Leona coughed awkwardly. "Well I should be going. Gail is expecting me at the store. That front window is a shambles and I have some ideas."

Ruby thanked her again, fearing for Violet and Gail's sanity once Leona got to them. As soon as she had gone, Ruby pulled the keyboard closer and searched for anything on the Swanson family. As she already knew, Agatha Swanson became the matriarch of the family when her mother died and after her father's death she had brought her much younger sister to the marital home and raised Meredith alongside her son.

They had stables, and decades ago were known for horse breeding, but the large farm had grown smaller as bits were sold off. The fields around them were still there but owned by other farmers now.

What kind of person had Agatha been? It sounded as though she had raised her son and Meredith as best she could in a world where her status and situation must have been in decline for some time. According to Gail, Agatha supported the church but did not concern herself much in any other aspect of the community.

There was no more information on Agatha and Ruby decided that she would have to speak more to Gail and possibly Linda to find out if they could add anything. However, she needed to discuss with her sisters whether she should tell Leona about the babies. Leona had been very forthcoming, but would illegitimate babies be too much to consider?

Chapter Seventeen

Closing time couldn't come soon enough for Ruby. She locked the doors and hurried to meet her sisters at the café where it was evident that Violet was as excited as she was about Jerome's news.

More intrigued with why Jerome had bought the run-down estate, Scarlett was also pleased that they had an invite. "Nate takes his job seriously and after warning us about going back to the house and trespassing, I wasn't sure how I'd stop you two from doing just that. Quite frankly, my sisters getting into more trouble—with or without me—was keeping me up at night. Being able to go to the estate legitimately is such a relief. I'll meet you outside."

How she knew that Ruby and Violet planned to go back to the estate by themselves since neither of them had mentioned it, Ruby wasn't sure, but it wouldn't be the first time their elder sister seemed to know what they were thinking.

Ruby paced the parking lot waiting for Scarlett to come out of the café's back door.

"Calm down," Violet told her.

Ruby snorted. "You're the one making weird noises."

It was true. Violet had a sound for every emotion and right now she was huffing which meant she was just as impatient to get to the estate.

Scarlett finally shut the door and ran down the steps with a bag slung over her shoulder. "Ready?"

Violet huffed once more. "No, we thought we'd have coffee first."

"Oh boy. Sarcasm. Good way to start the trip, Vi. You know I must leave the kitchen just so for the next day."

"We know," Violet and Ruby chorused.

"Good. Then stop fussing and let's go."

They piled into Ruby's car and before long were headed out of town in the direction of Harmony Beach. The estate was about halfway between there and Cozy Hollow. There was a car in front of the door.

"Looks like he's already here," Ruby's excitement at finally getting inside the house jumped up a notch.

"He has an exceptionally nice car for a principal," Scarlett noted.

"I think there is a great deal we don't know about Jerome," Ruby agreed.

Violet crossed her arms. "I don't care what state this place is in; he must have plenty of money to have bought it and that car is a giveaway."

"Please do not talk about money to him," Scarlett begged.

"Fine. But aren't you curious how a principal can afford an estate?"

"Of course, but that's not the point. We don't know him well enough to make it okay to dig into his personal life."

Violet shrugged. "Then I suggest we get to know him

better quickly. That way I can dig a little while we find out the Swanson's secrets at the same time."

"You two will be the death of me," Scarlett muttered.

"It will be fine. Jerome is really chilled out," Ruby assured her.

Scarlett rolled her eyes and walked sedately to the heavy door which stood open.

"Hello?" Ruby called into the wide entrance way.

They heard his footsteps before Jerome appeared down the far end and hurried toward them. "Hi! Thanks for coming. Do you want to wander at leisure, or shall I give you the grand tour?"

"The tour please," Violet spoke before Ruby could get a word in. "You'll know more about the place than we will."

He gave a slight bow and threw open the first door on the right. "According to the plans and the realtor, this is the front drawing room."

It had a massive threadbare red and black floral carpet square. From the lesser sun damaged and worn edges, it gave the impression that it had been something in its day. A fireplace with an elegant surround dominated the inside wall and it was clear by the patches on the carpet and wood just where furniture had stood.

"It's gorgeous," Violet gasped. "I think the house must be a similar age as Arthur Tully's place on Main Street."

"The mayor?" Jerome asked.

"That's right. He has a lot of the same features like that fireplace."

"It is impressive," Scarlett agreed.

Jerome grinned and led them across the hall. "The room opposite is a bedroom."

Violet poked her head inside the door and nodded. "Just like Arthur's."

"Come on down to the kitchen. I have the plans laid out for you on the old table which I think might be an original."

"Cool," Violet was aglow with eagerness and Scarlett was smiling indulgently. Both things made Ruby grin.

The four of them huddled around the plans in the huge kitchen that boasted a fireplace which could possibly spit roast a whole pig. Jerome pointed out the rooms he had already looked through.

"These are the first-floor bedrooms and reception rooms. There are more rooms on the second floor as well as a basement and an attic. It was a mess and even dustier before today. Plus the place is so big I could have missed a few things the first time around. I did get the roof, plumbing, and electrical checked." He grimaced. "I'm going to have to rewire, and the roof needs patching, so that affected the price. To be honest, that and the general condition was what made it affordable."

The sisters shot each other a glance which Jerome intercepted.

"Hah, there it is. I knew people would look at me weirdly when they heard about me buying the place."

"I'm so sorry, Jerome," Scarlett said. "It's none of our business how you managed it."

Ruby winced, recalling she had said those very words, and here she was intent on gleaning any snippet of the how and why of everything.

"You mean on a teacher and now a principal's salary?" He grinned and waved a hand at her. "No, it's fine. I need to get used to it and I know how the small-town rumor mill works by now. It will get out eventually and you three aren't as loose with the truth as some might be, so better it comes via you and your businesses."

"I think I'm flattered," Violet told him wryly.

He shrugged, but his eyes twinkled at her. "You'd think I'd be better with words. Here it is in a nutshell. A while back I started a tech company that I sold for a good price when I started teaching. I've been looking for something worthwhile to invest in other than shares, and I think I found it."

Violet tipped her head. "An old estate is worthwhile?"

Scarlett nudged her in the back and Violet swallowed.

"What I meant to say..."

"I want to open a school," he stated boldly and waited for that to sink in.

The sister's gasped. "A school?"

"Is it that weird? Okay, hear me out. Mainly I want to do this for the Harmony Beach children. The population is steadily growing and my plan is to start with the older children, which will lessen the load on the school." He nodded at Ruby. "You know they need more than they've been getting, so we'll teach all kinds of classes. Practical as well as the usual curriculum ones. They can learn to ride a horse or to bake. They can learn sewing or metalwork. Anything, really. The hard part, after the renovations, will be getting the right teachers."

"Jerome, that's simply awesome." Ruby sniffed, resisting the urge to hug him.

He gave a crooked grin. "I sure hope those are happy tears?"

She nodded and gulped back her emotions. "Anything that affords those children more opportunities is awesome and what you're describing sounds like the best kind of education for any child."

Ever the pessimist, Violet tutted. "Sure, but that's going to cost a lot to set up."

Ruby glared at her, but Jerome took it in his stride.

"I have an inkling of what I need from running Harmony Beach for the last few months and I've done a lot of research. I have a budget which probably won't cover everything I want but should be enough to get it off the ground. A dream must start somewhere, and I'm pretty sure you three know that."

"We do," Violet agreed suddenly changing tack as she often did when she thought about things. "And we also know that budgets can be stretched. If you need any help with sourcing furniture, let me know. I have a few contacts that deal in more modern items and my partner, Phin, will likely have other suggestions. You can always get a better deal if you buy in bulk."

He winked at her. "I must confess, the thought had crossed my mind that you would have some ideas. Perhaps you could let me know when you have some free time and we could visit showrooms together."

Ruby looked back and forth between them and bit her bottom lip to keep from blurting what her mind told her was a real possibility. Was something magic happening before their eyes? Was Jerome interested in Violet in more ways than a contact for furniture or as an assessor?

Staring down at the plans, she pretended to be more interested in those than watching the two of them flirting. This could be the beginning of a wonderful relationship for one of her unlucky-in-love sisters. But how could she prevent Violet from ruining it before it got started?

She glanced up to find Scarlett's eyebrows knitted together and she shot her a questioning look. They nodded at each other and quickly looked away. Having them notice was a sure-fire way for Violet to get anti-Jerome and clearly they were of the same mindset. They didn't have to speak to appreciate that the only way this might blossom was to pretend to be oblivious and, when the opportunity arose, nudge them in the right direction.

In the seconds that lapsed, Violet's cheeks had turned pink. She coughed and backed up to the door. "I'm sure we can sort something out. Well, I guess you have plenty to do right now and I really don't mind looking around by myself."

"That's okay. I can't do much without any tools and as I told Ruby, I'd really like your opinion on some pieces I bought from Edgar Swanson."

"Oh. Well, lead on. Are you two coming?" Violet's steely gaze suggested they should do just that.

"I'd like to look downstairs if that's okay?" Ruby said with a straight face.

"I'll go with Ruby to make sure she doesn't get lost," Scarlett joked. "You know what she's like."

Jerome pointed across the room. "The internal door is over there in the corner."

Violet narrowed her eyes, but didn't say anything and Ruby turned away, listening for retreating footsteps as she opened the door and felt around for the light switch.

When she turned, Scarlett put a finger to her lips and they quietly descended to an even dustier level, avoiding the handrail coated in cobwebs. At the bottom was a large room and off this were four doors.

"Don't you think it's cute that Jerome is keen on Violet?" Ruby whispered.

"Too cute." Scarlett chuckled. "She's going to hate us for noticing."

"I really like him. I hope she doesn't scare him off," Ruby mused.

"You know Violet. The only men she really respects are Phin, Nate, and Alex."

"That's because they're taken, which makes them safe."

"Very true." Scarlett shivered. "Do we really have to look around down here? It gives me the creeps."

"Once Jerome modernizes the lighting it will be fine. Come on, we're here so we may as well see if there are any secrets hidden in these rooms."

"Arrgh! I completely forgot about the Swansons and those notes for a moment."

"Well I didn't," Ruby told her emphatically. "Someone wrote those notes in this house and now we have an opportunity to find out if they were for real, or if it was a hoax."

"At least you're entertaining both realities."

"Unlike Nate," Ruby said caustically.

Scarlett blinked. "That's not like you."

"Sorry. I know he has a lot on and a ghost from the past isn't what he needs, but this nagging feeling that it's exactly what I think it is won't go away."

Scarlett sighed. "Fine. You go first."

Chapter Eighteen

The room housed a bleak laundry in one corner. By the window next to it, Ruby could see that the door on their left led outside. The second door was straight ahead and required some jiggling to get it open. It was swollen along the bottom as if there had been a flood on this floor and took both women to push it open far enough to slip inside.

"A wine cellar," Scarlett pronounced as she walked the length of the room holding her phone in front of her with the torch app on. "Sadly, empty except for the shelves."

Ruby tested a couple of these with a push and found them fixed to the floor. "Do you think Edgar drank everything or took it with him?"

"Perhaps a bit of both," Scarlett mused. "Although, it was probably gone long ago. I really can't imagine that anyone came in here recently. Not with the door the way it is."

Ruby nodded. "I think this floor must have originally held the kitchen and they've moved it upstairs at some stage. She moved onto the third door. Inside was a tiny bathroom.

It held a toilet, shower and handbasin. "Don't you find it odd that there are no cupboards in here? Where would you stock towels and toiletries?"

Scarlett shrugged. "I imagine that there are plenty of bathrooms upstairs. Go ahead and check that last door so we can get out of here."

Humoring her sister, Ruby turned the handle. It didn't budge. "It's locked. Jerome must have a key. You would have thought he'd insist on going through every space to make sure it wasn't rotten and beyond repair."

"Well we can't get in, so I guess we go back up." Scarlett took no pains to hide her eagerness.

Ruby wasn't 100% sure if it was due to the dirtiness of the place, or to see how Violet was butchering a potential budding romance. She had to admit to being curious about that too, but she was more curious about what was behind door four.

The others weren't back, so they meandered through the rooms on this level. There were plenty of them.

Ruby sighed. "I bet Violet is having the time of her life."

"You think?" Scarlett grinned. "Old stuff and Jerome do seem like a winning combination."

"Shush! If she hears you she'll have a fit."

Scarlett chuckled as they walked in and out of several rooms. "What are we looking for exactly?"

"A sign that Meredith lived here."

"But we know she did."

Ruby marched across the nearest room and stared out the window where she could see the graveyard. "I meant, when did she live in the house? Was it from the day she arrived until her death? And most importantly, did she have a genuine concern for her well-being?"

"Well, I'm not sure you're going to get all that from an empty room. Anyway, Edgar said she died elsewhere."

"Elsewhere is a big place." Ruby mused. "Why can't we find any mention of her death? She turned back to the door and frowned. "If she lived on the main floor with the rest of the family and she was mentally troubled like Edgar said, they'd be worried about her wandering the countryside and getting lost. If she wanted to get outside, but they didn't want her to leave the house, it stands to reason that the door would at least have a lock."

"Did you notice if any of the rooms had locks?"

Ruby nodded. "I checked every one on this floor and none of them did. Unlike the one downstairs. Also, it wouldn't be ideal to have her room near the front door, or anywhere they might entertain visitors."

"That makes sense, except for Edgar not appearing to be fond of visitors. Although, I guess his mom may have felt differently."

"Maybe," Ruby conceded. "Let's check upstairs."

They made their way up the threadbare staircase and along a long landing where there were many more bedrooms which Ruby bypassed. "I think we should start at the back this time."

"Okay. At least it's reasonably clean up here."

"I guess it would have been hard to maintain every room when he was on his own." Ruby conceded as she turned the handle of the last door. It opened easily and she walked inside the empty room. It was large as were all the rooms on this floor and it was easy to see that a bed head had rested against the far wall in the middle of the room. Unfaded flooring showed where the other pieces of furniture had been. "It's just a normal room."

Scarlett tutted. "Don't sound too disappointed."

121

"You're right. Finding evidence of a woman being tied up, or something like that, would have been terrible."

Scarlett wrapped an arm around her shoulders. "I get it. You want to solve the mystery. I've been there, but maybe this time there isn't anything to solve. It really could have been a joke between friends."

"I get the impression that Meredith, like Edgar, didn't have any friends."

"I think you might be right about Edgar, but we can't be certain about Meredith."

Ruby tilted her head. "Leona seemed to think she wanted friends, but once she was home-schooled she didn't see anyone from the town."

"If she lost touch as she said she did, then Leona can't be sure that no one stopped by to visit Meredith at home," Scarlett said reasonably.

"That's the trouble," Ruby groaned. "No one seems certain of anything when it comes to Meredith, and I don't know how to shake the feeling that I must do more."

"We haven't finished looking around yet. Maybe Jerome has suggestions of likely hiding spots. Sometimes in old places like this there would be alcoves, nooks and crannies that might not be obvious."

Scarlett was so level-headed, that Ruby perked up a little as they checked the rest of the rooms on this floor. They were mostly all the same size and the level of disuse was similar—except for two rooms.

These were at the start of the landing and much bigger than the others. The one on the left was clearly a woman's room. The wallpaper was various shades of pink depicting roses in bloom. Ruby couldn't resist opening the large empty wardrobe. The doors pushed back concertina fashion so that the person looking at their clothes had a panoramic view. She got a whiff of mothballs, a smell she wasn't partial to, and quickly shut them.

The lights on the wall at each side of the bed looked newer than she would expect, as if they were a recent addition. A door at the back of the room led to an ensuite. It was completely tiled and set up for an invalid with handrails by the toilet and the shower. If it had a bath at any stage this had been removed and, if necessary, there was plenty of space for a wheelchair.

She had assumed Agatha had died of old age and made a mental note to check on Agatha's infirmity and cause of death.

Across the hall the other room was more masculine with lots of dark wood paneling. It also had an ensuite, but this was old and tired.

"I think these must have been Edgar and his mom's rooms."

Scarlett nodded. "Absolutely. The rest of the place hasn't been touched in decades but they both look like they've had a lot more attention. Except for Edgar's bathroom."

"Ruby? Scarlett?" Violet's voice came from downstairs.

"Oops. She sounds desperate," Scarlett grinned.

"Coming," Ruby called on her way down.

Their sister waited at the bottom, wearing an exasperated look.

"Sorry, I didn't think we'd been gone so long. Have you finished looking at furniture?" Ruby asked innocently.

"Ages ago. We've been twiddling our thumbs waiting for you two to surface."

"There's no hurry," Jerome interjected. "It's been great to have more eyes on the place. I dither between excitement and fear that I've bitten off more than I can chew."

"The place is amazing," Violet stated. "Don't let anyone tell you this isn't a wonderful venture. I'm sure you'll be successful with the school."

"Thanks for the vote of confidence, Violet. It means a lot coming from you."

Once more, Violet turned a pretty shade of pink. "You're welcome. We should be going." The words came out in a choked way and she all but ran to the front door.

"Did you manage to see everything you wanted to?" Jerome asked.

Ruby noticed the frown he directed at Violet and her hurried escape. The poor man looked out of his depth.

"Almost. All except the room in the basement."

He nodded. "Ah, yes. I forgot that was still locked. Edgar had lost the key, but he assured me they are now all in a drawer in the kitchen if you want to look inside while you're here."

"Really?" That would be fantastic if you can find it."

"Let me check if one of them fits. It will be a good test, because he was so flustered about the keys, I thought he might forget."

"Don't tell me you didn't check all the rooms before you signed your life away?" Asked Violet who had returned trying to hide her frustration.

Every room except one," he admitted slightly shame faced. "It's a big place as I'm sure you can appreciate and it took a very long time when you consider there are a lot of outbuildings and the barn."

Violet shrugged. "Then I'm sure there isn't anything important in there, right?"

"Please Violet," Ruby begged. "It won't take long."

Violet groaned. "Okay. Just make sure it doesn't."

Ruby didn't argue. Following Jerome to the kitchen, she

wondered why Violet returned and figured she must have heard about the locked room. None of them could resist that. Unless it was spending a little more time with Jerome.

Jerome pulled a large metal key ring from a drawer. It had a dozen or more keys dangling from it and some of them looked very old.

"You won't have to carry that bunch around with you every day when the place opens, will you?" Violet asked.

He laughed. "No way. They weigh a ton. It's a short-term thing until I figure out what they all fit. Otherwise I can see myself chasing the right one if I leave them behind while I'm still discovering locked rooms."

"You mean there were other rooms locked besides this one?"

"Quite a few on the upper floor were and these down here. Apparently, Edgar had the place cleaned and locked the doors when they were done so he didn't end up paying twice."

Ruby glanced around her in the gloomy light of the old bulb overhead. "Judging by the cobwebs, they weren't the best cleaners."

Jerome shrugged. "I think it was more of a cursory dust to make it sale-able, but you must remember the place was on the market for a long time. Without continued maintenance, it was bound to look worse for wear. Like I said, that worked in my favor when negotiating the sale price."

He crouched at the lock and then studied the selection. Running his finger along the keys he spied one that seemed to be a possibility. It didn't fit, but he looked like he knew what he wanted now and tried another three before he had success.

Ruby's heart did a little flip when he pushed the door open. She wasn't sure what she expected to find, but it wasn't walls the color of the sky. A darker patch, the size of a window, covered the back wall. Intrigued, she moved closer and touched the paint. It was dry of course, but it was fresher than the rest of the walls and looked out of place. The room was devoid of furniture and unlike the upper floors, there were few marks to distinguish where any might have been, or if indeed any had been in here. The lack of sunlight in the internal room would certainly be a contributing factor for having no faded carpet.

She became aware of Violet standing in the doorway, arms folded, tapping her foot. Ruby ignored her sister and walked around the room peering into each corner. A picture of a woman stuck in her mind. With long flowing blonde hair, her figment wore a white nightgown. Ruby had never seen a picture of Meredith, so it was pure imagination, yet she also felt a palpable presence which had nothing to do with Violet's annoyance.

A slight lump under her left foot made Ruby pause mid-stride and her breath came faster.

Chapter Nineteen

A foot away from the back wall, Ruby rubbed her shoe back and forth. There was no doubt that the floor beneath the threadbare carpet was not even. Kneeling she ran her hand across the area.

"What is it?" Violet asked, suddenly interested.

"There's a small lump here."

Jerome knelt beside her. "Could be a warped floorboard."

"It probably is, but could we take a look?" Ruby couldn't keep the excitement from her voice.

"Of course. Everything needs replacing anyway." Jerome crawled to the edge of the carpet and lifted the corner. It pulled back easily and he rolled it toward Ruby who shuffled back to give him space.

As soon as the area was exposed, she pounced to where the wood was raised at a join and pushed her slim fingers into the slight gap there. Unfortunately, the wood was wedged in tightly.

"Let me have a try." Jerome pulled out a pocket knife and opened the small blade. Poking the tip into the gap he jiggled until it was inserted to the hilt. He pressed down on the handle, then gave it a whack with his other hand. The wood lifted and a small wedge flew out.

Ruby held her breath while Jerome manhandled the rest of a foot long piece of wood and dropped it on the floor beside him. The long rectangular gap he'd exposed was not empty. A much-used pen, judging by the bend in the middle and the chewed end, sat on a sheaf of pages.

"These look like they come from the books which were donated to the library." Ruby was surprisingly breathless and realized she must have held it for a long time. Swallowing hard she licked her dry lips. "This must be Meredith's room."

"It could be one she had access to," Violet noted. "You've assumed she wrote the notes, but we can't know for sure if it was her handwriting."

Ruby blinked. "We do know Meredith had issues. Edgar let it slip, remember? Other than Meredith, I don't think there was anyone other than Edgar and Agatha Swanson living here for years. And as far as we know, only Meredith hasn't been seen in recent times. This room is in a similar state to Edgar's, so we can surmise that it was used more recently than the others in the house. It would be the perfect place to hide someone and yet still have access to them as needed."

"I understand why you think the family believed she was a threat to herself or others," Scarlett said carefully. "Only, Nate would say that we can't know the mindset of the family or how they lived to be certain. And there doesn't seem to be a way of finding out."

"That's where I think you're both wrong. I mean I get that you're playing Devil's advocate here, but you've forgotten that Edgar knew his aunt and took care of her as well as his mother. He had to know where Meredith lived—and how she lived."

Her sisters stood behind her as Ruby took a handkerchief from her pocket and pulled the items from the hole. Underneath them something sparkled.

"A locket!" Ruby dropped the papers and pen on the floor and carefully picked up the locket with the cloth. She opened her hand and allowed the chain to fall over her palm as she rocked the locket back and forth on the cloth.

"Go ahead and open it," Jerome told her.

Her fingers itched at the suggestion, but she held it out to him. "Are you sure, you don't want to?"

"It doesn't belong to me. I'm happy to return it to the rightful owner, but we can't do that if we don't find out who it really belongs to."

"What about fingerprints?" Scarlett asked.

Leaning over Ruby, Violet shook her head. "It's so small, I doubt that the police could get anything clear from it."

Ruby gave that a second to sink in, then took a deep breath. Her fingers shook a little as she put a fingernail into the groove and flicked the latch. It was a little stiff but didn't require much effort to open it. A picture of a young woman was fixed into the right-hand side. On the left a man stared at the camera, or the person behind it. His eyes were soft, but he wasn't young. There was something familiar about him.

"Do you recognize them?" Jerome asked.

Ruby shook her head. "The photos aren't exactly clear. They could be anyone."

"He looks a little old to be a boyfriend."

Violet glanced at him. "Why does he have to be a boyfriend?"

"Unless it's a parent or a sibling, why else would he be in her locket?"

"Are we sure this is Meredith's?" Scarlett asked.

Ruby peered at the grainy picture. "Pretty sure."

"Why don't we get it confirmed before you take this any further? I suggest we ask Leona before tackling Edgar."

"Good idea," Ruby agreed. "Edgar won't be happy with any digging we do, but after her visit to me it seems that Leona wants this mystery to be solved. She may even feel guilty about not staying in touch with Meredith."

Violet raised an eyebrow. "I can't imagine she would admit to that. Anyway, Edgar's reluctance is mighty suspicious."

"Having ghosts in the closet isn't easy for anyone," Ruby reminded her.

"What are your plans after you speak to Leona?" Jerome asked with interest.

Ruby shrugged. "Nothing's changed. I still want to know what happened to Meredith, so I'll speak to whoever I need to."

He frowned. "She is dead though, isn't she?"

"That's just it. We can't find any record of her death."

Wide-eyed he took another look at the locket. "So she could be alive?"

Ruby shrugged. "It's not impossible, she'd be age 65."

Jerome simply stared and Ruby made a strangled sound. He made her realize that somewhere along the way she had unwittingly discarded the notion.

"I had my suspicions, yet I still accepted Edgar's word for her death! Even after we couldn't find a record."

"You immediately went to foul play," Scarlett said ruefully.

"Tell me you didn't?"

Her sister raised a fine eyebrow. "I did, but it was based on what you'd told us."

"That's right," Violet agreed. "Although, we always felt that none of this was above board."

"Or easily explained," Jerome agreed. "I have to admit I am fascinated by how your minds work." He waved a hand at the treasures. "All this because of a couple of notes."

"It does sound ridiculous when you say it like that," Violet agreed.

"No, I don't think it's ridiculous. I think it would be awesome to solve a case. Especially one that could be easily brushed under the carpet."

Ruby snorted and the others looked down at the rolled bundle on the floor.

"Let's keep looking around the room in case this wasn't the only hidey-hole."

Chapter Twenty

They didn't find any other secret stashes, but Ruby was more convinced she had to get to the bottom of this, despite the hiccups they were experiencing. If she hadn't pushed, this room mightn't be touched for months or years and Jerome would potentially never have found the paper and pen.

As luck would have it she was at the bakery counter the next day when Leona came in with Linda.

Scarlett nudged her. "I think you should see to them."

Ruby didn't need asking twice. Taking a pad and pen she went to take their orders. "Good morning ladies. You're out early today. Are the others joining you for another meeting?"

"Not this time," Leona said archly.

"Gail's busy with the store and Olivia said she had something to do," Linda replied and winced when Leona grumbled about loose lips sinking ships.

"Oh, that's a shame. What can I get you?"

They ordered and Ruby took a step closer. "Would you mind looking at a picture, Mrs. Wolf?"

Leona stared hard at her. "I beg your pardon?"

"I'm sorry to trouble you, but I found a locket with a couple of pictures in it and Scarlett suggested you would be the perfect person to know if it was of one of our fellow residents so I could return it to its rightful owner." Ruby crossed her fingers behind her back at the fabrication.

The woman nodded regally. "I do know most people in town, so it's likely I'll be able to help."

"Thank you." Ruby took the locket from her pocket and opened it. She handed it to Leona who squinted at the picture on the left.

"Goodness, I haven't seen that face for years. It's Meredith Denton. She must have been about sixteen here; about the time we were in the choir."

Ruby was so excited; she almost took a seat. While desperately wanting every detail, if Leona wasn't handled right she could be tricky, especially with Linda as an audience. By the pointed look sent her way, it seemed obvious that Leona didn't want to discuss their prior meeting. "I meant to ask about that. Do you still sing?"

"Not in front of people. Something happens to your voice as you get older." Leona grimaced as if this left a bad taste in her mouth.

"Yes, it got all scratchy, didn't it," Linda added helpfully.

Leona stiffened. "It's not that bad, but one doesn't like to let anyone down by not giving a complete performance."

"I'm sure you still have a lovely voice," Ruby cajoled her. "Were you all friends with Meredith at school?"

"We were—friendly. She came from money and, though it's tacky to discuss such things these days, we stuck to our own circles back then."

"That's right," Linda added. "We weren't rich like the

Swansons and it showed. They never went anywhere without wearing their Sunday best." She giggled. "I'm sure they had a different Sunday best for every day."

"Hmmpf," Leona grumped. "Are we getting our order anytime soon?"

"My apologies for keeping you. I just find our history so interesting and you know so much about it. Could I ask quickly if you knew the man opposite?"

Leona made another impatient sound but drew the locket close to her face to get a better look. "Hmmm. Looks like Ambrose to me."

"Ambrose? I've never heard that name before."

"You've never met the minister?" Leona scoffed. "I find that hard to believe."

Ruby gaped. "The minister?"

"Coffee?" Leona answered waspishly.

Ruby hurried to the counter and thrust the order at Scarlett then hissed. "The man in the picture is the minister according to Leona."

"No way!" Violet squawked from the doorway.

"And Leona confirmed the woman's picture is Meredith when she was about age sixteen."

They stared at each other for a few seconds.

"Do you think he was the father of her children?" Ruby finally managed to whisper.

"A minister?" Scarlett gasped. "Surely not."

"Then why would she have a picture of him? Let's look at it again, Rubes." Violet insisted.

"Not here. Leona's watching us." Ruby indicated with her chin the glare directed at them.

Scarlett sighed. "I better get those coffees out to them before she throws a fit."

"You do that while we get the food, then we can meet

back in the kitchen." Ruby's fingers itched and she hoped no one else came in for a few minutes.

They worked in harmony as if the last year had not changed anything and soon they were huddled around the locket again as far back in the kitchen as they could get.

Ruby pressed one of the pictures and it moved. "The minister's picture has been roughly cut to fit and there are more pictures underneath." One at a time, she gently removed the pictures from the locket to find the originals underneath. "I wonder if these are Meredith's parents."

Scarlett chewed her bottom lip. "The woman does look a lot like her."

"She does," Ruby agreed. "You don't think it's Meredith when she's older?"

"No." Violet shook her head firmly. "Look at the paper. It's much older than the one used in the front one and has been hand painted."

Ruby was impressed and reminded once more that Violet was not only a darn good baker. She knew her stuff and was so confident about sharing her expertise without showing off. "Okay, if we're agreed that this is Meredith's and she was kept in that room against her will, what do we do next?"

"Please do not go to the minister and accuse him of anything," Scarlett begged.

"Give us some credit," Violet muttered.

The raised eyebrow shushed her and Ruby decided not to voice an opinion about that. She wasn't about to race to the church, but she had been thinking that a visit to the minister was a must—at some stage.

Scarlett eyed them both. "You should get to work. We can talk about this tonight and make a plan."

Violet shrugged. "Not if Ruby's at the diner we can't."

"I'll pop in to make sure Alex is okay then come right home," Ruby assured them before she hurried out the door, not waiting for Violet.

As soon as she had a moment she'd check the internet for anything she could find on the minister. It didn't matter to her if Meredith had an affair, or with who. She just wanted to know what happened to her. Was she dead and buried? If so, where? And was the minister involved in her disappearance? If not, then someone had to know where she was living. That someone could also be the minister. And then there was Edgar. What was he hiding?

She almost ran to the diner and knew she wasn't as attentive to Alex as she should have been. Her fingers itched for the keyboard and her mind whirled with possibilities. What possible reason could Edgar have to say that Meredith was dead if she was alive? And was a minister allowed a girlfriend?

"Ruby? Did you hear what I asked?"

Alex's voice filtered through her pondering and she looked up guiltily. "Sorry. I was miles away. What did you say?"

"It's okay. You must have a busy day ahead. Go on now, I will see you later."

She kissed him hard and he looked at her searchingly.

"Is everything alright?"

"Can't a woman, who won't see her fiancé all day give him a kiss?"

"This woman can anytime she wants," he squeezed her to him then turned her around and pushed her to the door. "No more though, or I will forget what I am doing."

She grinned all the way to the library, but once inside Ruby was completely focused on the mystery. Before she searched for more information on the minister, she looked up Meredith Denton for the umpteenth time.

No one could mess with facts and figures and she confirmed that Meredith Denton was born in 1958—sixteen years after Agatha. Their mother, Sarah Denton died a couple of days after giving birth.

It seemed likely that sixteen-year-old Agatha became a substitute for the motherless baby and when their father passed away it would have been natural for Meredith to come live with Agatha.

The dates made things very interesting. Edgar was only three years younger than Meredith. Therefore, the close relationship they had was most likely due to being brought up more as brother and sister than aunt and nephew. If they were as close as everyone intimated then surely he would want to know she was okay—or visit her grave.

Thinking of graves made Ruby ponder that finding Agatha's may help in some way. She wasn't sure how, but it was one more piece in the puzzle and at least it was handy. That's if the records were correct and Edgar hadn't lied about his mother being buried in town.

Chapter Twenty-One

I t had taken all Ruby's patience to get through the day at a job she loved, which spoke of how caught up in the case she was.

She should be at the diner, but this was the only time she could visit the graveyard so she had allowed herself half an hour to search for Agatha's grave.

After slipping through a squeaky gate she walked around the back of the church and studied the somewhat haphazard lines of headstones. The ones closest were old and though some were still well tended, others had fallen into disrepair.

"Ruby!"

She clutched her throat and turned—to find Gail Norman right behind her.

The compact woman's eyes widened. "Are you okay? You look like you've seen a ghost."

Ruby managed a weak smile. "You scared the heck out of me. I wasn't expecting to see anyone here at this time of day."

"People come to pay their respects at all kinds of times."

"I suppose. Is that what you're doing?"

"Not today," Gail said lightly. "Leona, Linda, and I take turns tidying the graves. Are you here to visit your mom?"

That only added to Ruby's guilt, since she hadn't considered visiting her mom while she was here. The sisters usually visited together and spent some time most weekends. "I'll stop by, but I was actually looking for Agatha Swanson's grave."

Gail nodded. "Ah, I should have known. Come on then, I'll show you where she is."

Ruby followed her to the far end of the graveyard where the newest graves were.

Gail stopped in front of a reasonable sized, but not flashy headstone. "Here she is. I was just a child the only time I went to her house and I remember thinking how attractive she was. She was very nice to me and got Edgar to show me around the house. The size of the library impressed me and I believe she brought many of the books from her parents' house."

"Maybe at the same time as Meredith came to live with her?"

"Possibly. Agatha did inherit everything when her parents passed and according to my mom, they were very wealthy."

"That is interesting. I thought their wealth was from the Swanson side of the family."

"Anyone my age or older can tell you the Swansons once had a great deal of money, and that the men in the family liked to spend it. It was common knowledge."

"I did read about the sale of land. Are you saying that two generations blew the family fortune?" Ruby prompted. Having looked everywhere for more details on the family and coming up empty-handed this was fascinating. Obviously, the Swansons had been adept at keeping gossip to a minimum, but Gail was family and Ruby could kick herself for not asking more questions earlier.

Gail lowered her voice. "My mom told me that Robert's father set up a distillery and it burned down. Apparently, he had no insurance. He then decided to go into dairy farming and some disease wiped out the herd. After that he planted crops that anyone could have told him wouldn't grow in this area. I guess some of it was bad luck, but mostly it was lack of research and common sense."

"I imagine that Agatha's money was sucked into the coffers."

Gail nodded. "They would have needed her money to carry on as if nothing was amiss. Keeping up appearances was very important to Agatha."

This made Ruby wonder if this hadn't been the catalyst for keeping the family away from prying eyes. With little money for new clothes and up keep of the estate it would have been apparent that they were struggling.

Gail was watching her curiously and Ruby smiled. "This has been very enlightening."

"Does it help at all?"

"I'm not sure how just yet," Ruby admitted, "but you can't follow a lead properly if you don't have all the details and you've certainly filled in many of the blanks. What about Edgar's management of the estate?"

"I honestly think that when he finally got his hands on it, there was nothing he could do to save it."

"How do you know that?"

Gail looked around furtively. "One afternoon a few months ago, I was weeding under the minister's office and heard him talking to Edgar about the condition of the estate and that he should be glad to get rid of it. He said Agatha's father-in-law wasn't good with money and it was obvious that the place was in decline years ago. He added that Robert wasn't much of a farmer either. Then he said something about Edgar being able to live a much simpler life in his cottage. From that I can only assume that they went through Agatha's money as well. The minister was a bit crasser about it, if I'm honest, and Edgar sounded very upset about the situation."

This was more excellent information and Ruby encouraged Gail to continue. "Selling his home would make him sad, and when his mom was alive she must have been upset to have their circumstances change so drastically."

Gail snorted. "I would say so. They stopped donating money to different causes years ago and there weren't any lavish parties for decades. Not that I think Agatha was keen on them anyway. I shouldn't talk ill of the dead, especially not a family member, but she was a bit of a snob. I don't think there were many around Cozy Hollow she felt were in her peer group."

While it all sounded plausible, not that she thought Gail had exactly embellished what she heard, there were still things that didn't add up. You said you hadn't spent much time in Agatha's company. What about Meredith?"

Pink cheeked, Gail stared at the ground. "We were cousins, but I was the poor one and not really considered friend material." She glanced up. "Don't get me wrong, Meredith didn't see me that way, but her mother certainly did. I was okay to speak to Meredith at school, but not to visit. That's why it was odd that Agatha left me anything."

Ruby had considered this. "I'd say the books were an oversight in Edgar's haste to get rid of the place. Agatha was probably thinking of something lesser than all those books."

"I dare say you're right." Gail gave a mischievous grin.

"Violet thinks we will get a good return on the ones in the store."

"I'm so glad for you. I must go, but can I ask one more thing? Were you friendly with Edgar?"

Gail shrugged. "To be honest, he didn't care for anyone except Meredith. Leona chatted with both of them quite frequently and was very fond of Meredith. The thing I remember most, is they simply didn't talk about Agatha or the estate."

"It is very strange. I never thought to ask him, and I'm sure he wouldn't have said, but do you know where Edgar lives now?"

Gail pointed across a field opposite. "He bought the old cottage behind that tree line. It's not much and was abandoned for years, but perhaps it was all he could afford."

Ruby stared at the trees, noting that it was also handy to town for when he went to the diner to pick up his meals. Meals? How many did he get at one time—for how many people? She would have to ask Alex.

"Thanks Gail for taking the time to tell me all this. I need to get to the diner, but you've given me a lot to think about."

"No problem." Gail shivered. "I just wish I hadn't seen the minister looking at us through his window." She shielded her mouth with a hand. "He's a grumpy so and so at the best of times, so he's bound to think badly of our meeting."

Ruby resisted the urge to look. "I know and I'm sorry if he takes it out on you that I'm here. Anyway, thanks again."

Now her head was bursting with thoughts of the minister, Edgar's cottage, and how controlling Agatha had been. Sadly, the late Mrs. Swanson hadn't been able to control the other men in her life as she might have preferred.

Maybe that was why she had been so hard on her son. Since there was a wedge between them and Edgar's loyalty was with Meredith, it stood to reason that he would have done whatever he needed to make sure his aunt was taken care of.

She walked back to Main Street and was near the diner when she saw Edgar leaving. He carried a bag to a shabby white car and placed the bag on the passenger seat.

Then he drove toward the church.

Chapter Twenty-Two

From the kitchen Alex gave her a grin as soon as he saw her. Ruby nodded at Lexi who was taking an order at the back of the diner.

Alex gave her a quick kiss on the cheek before placing a steak on the grill. "Do you want me to cook something for you?"

"Not tonight, thanks. I just saw Edgar Swanson leaving."

"Yes, he picked up his order." Alex shrugged. "He never eats here, but I guess he likes the food."

"Does he buy dinner often?" she asked.

"Not often. He does pick up a dessert a few times a week. I am very lucky that you and Scarlett taught me how to make them as they sell very well."

He sounded so proud, and she smiled. "That's good. He must have a sweet tooth."

"Who?"

"Edgar Swanson."

"A lot of sweet tooths." Alex chuckled at his joke. "He must eat fast tonight as he is going to a meeting in Destiny."

"Why would he have a meeting in Destiny at night?"

"I did not ask. Is it important?"

"No. I was just curious."

Alex looked up and frowned. "That bothers me."

She forced a laugh and watched him expertly flip eggs and plate up the food. "No need to worry. I was merely thinking about how he lives now that he no longer has staff to cook and clean for him."

"No one should have slaves. We should all cook and clean."

Her heart did a flip. Living together once they were married was sounding like it would be easier than she'd considered. "I'm so glad to hear you say that. Sharing housework sounds perfect to me."

"We will share everything," he told her as he put the plate on the pass and tapped a bell.

"I've got some things to research online so I'm heading home. We can catch up for lunch tomorrow if that's okay?"

"That will be nice." He smiled and pulled her into his arms so he could kiss her properly.

Her cheeks flamed and she was a little breathless when he eventually let her go. "That was better than nice."

"I was hoping you would think so and that you will think of it often until I see you again."

"It will be less than twenty-four hours, but I could never forget how much I love you."

He grinned and stirred a large pot. "You should go now before I kiss you again."

Lexie chuckled as she collected the order and Alex blushed which made Ruby laugh all the way back to the library where she collected her car.

Back at the cottage Bob and George mobbed her as soon as she got through the back door. When Ruby was going to be home later, Violet often brought the pets home, so they wouldn't have to hang around the diner.

Violet was preparing dinner and barely glanced at her. "I thought you'd be at the diner a while longer."

"I decided that I had something more important to do."

Violet glanced up. "More important than spending time with Alex? I am intrigued."

Casually Ruby leaned on the counter. "After I closed the library I stopped by the cemetery to find Agatha's grave and Gail was there. We discussed the Swanson's a little more. She told me that Edgar has a place not far from the church."

"That's interesting. I thought he'd moved away."

Ruby nodded. "I think it was an assumption we all made. He was struggling financially so maybe a run-down cottage is all he could afford. How do you feel about taking a drive there?"

Violet motioned at the sink. "I'm in the middle of making dinner."

"Right. It's just that I saw Edgar drive out of town and I'd like to look around his place before he gets back."

Violet snorted and continued washing vegetables. "Nate wouldn't like that."

"No he wouldn't, but he and Scarlett are having dinner at Nate's place tonight so they don't need to know."

Violet dropped the vegetables in the sink. "All right. Let's go."

Ruby grinned. They weren't scared of Nate or Scarlett,

but it was best not to poke the bear in either of them if they could help it.

Town was five minutes away and Ruby found the long driveway to the cottage easy enough. She drove slowly until they came to a slight bend. "Let's go on foot from here," she suggested.

When Violet didn't argue they crept around several straggly trees to find the cottage in worse condition than Ruby had imagined. Vines grew up the walls and around a chimney. The gardens were unkempt, although it looked like someone had begun to till soil for planting down the side of the house.

Violet tutted. "How could he bear this place after that huge estate?"

"Having all that space to roam and then moving into what looks like two-bedrooms must feel like living in a shoe-box," Ruby agreed. "Come on, let's have a look before he gets back."

"You don't intend to break in do you?" her sister asked warily.

"Of course not. Unless he left a window open," Ruby teased. Although, she couldn't say with any certainty that she wouldn't be sorely tempted to explore further if the opportunity arose.

Fortunately, she didn't have to worry about winding up in jail for breaking and entering, since everything was shut including all the curtains.

"If we didn't know from Gail that this is where he lives, I would think the place was abandoned."

"I know what you mean, Vi. Hey, there's the trash can. Shall we?"

Violet wrinkled her nose. "You go right ahead. I don't even know what you're looking for."

"Evidence." Ruby said and lifted the lid off the trash bin.

Violet peered inside before taking a step back. "You'll need to expand on that."

"Evidence that he knows where Meredith is."

"So you think Edgar, a reasonably intelligent man, wrote it on a piece of paper or a cereal box and then put it in his trash?"

"Quit with the sarcasm. You know very well that evidence can be more obscure than that."

"I do, but the man just lost his family home and before that his mom. We don't have to like him to feel sorry for him and give him the benefit of the doubt."

Ruby sighed at Violet playing the devils' advocate. "He's the connection—the only one who could know the truth about the graves and Meredith."

"Other than the minister and the knitting group."

Ruby delicately pulled takeout boxes from the diner to one side. "We asked them all and no one would, or could, help with Meredith's whereabouts."

"Look, I get that you're frustrated…"

"Insulin!" Ruby yelled excitedly.

"What?"

Ruby pulled a tissue from her pocket and plucked a small bottle from the trash. "Edgar is a diabetic."

"Okay, Sherlock. Lots of people are. Why do you look like you've solved the puzzle?"

Ruby pointed at the containers. "Edgar buys desserts regularly from the diner."

"But if he is insulin dependent, he can't eat them." Violet's eyes lit up. "Which means he's buying them for someone else."

"Exactly! Leona told me that Meredith loved sweet things. This is evidence."

"Are you going to tell Nate? You realise it's not enough? Edgar could have a friend or even a girlfriend who likes desserts."

"Sure, but Edgar isn't known for having friends." She saw Violets' look and nodded. "It's flimsy, but it is something. I won't spoil their date, but tomorrow, I'm going to ask Nate to check this place out. There's a lot to consider, but it's time to get out of here before anyone spots us hanging around."

Violet merely nodded, already lost in thought.

Chapter Twenty-Three

The next day, Ruby had been flat out with the local school and hadn't had a chance to contact Nate and Scarlett was in a funny mood that morning. She was putting away returned books prior to closing the library when the large door opened and in walked the minister. Her mouth dropped open and she just managed to snap it shut before he saw her astonishment.

"Good afternoon, Minister. This is unexpected."

His thick eyebrows joined together. "I don't believe that's quite true, Ms. Finch. Is it?"

She flushed. "It's true that I didn't expect to see you here."

He gave a slight nod. "Very well. I heard that you've been asking questions of my parishioners."

"As I'm not familiar with who all your parishioners might be, I can only think you're alluding to the café customers."

His mouth pursed. "To be clear, I was talking about Mrs. Wolf and Ms. Night who informed me that you had indeed been subjecting them to sensitive questioning."

"I was talking to Leona and Linda in the café," Ruby admitted with no apology. She had nothing to be embarrassed about and his pompous attitude was frankly annoying. "I don't see how asking about how or when other residents came to Cozy Hollow could be deemed sensitive."

His eyes narrowed. "My office overlooks the cemetery so please don't deny that you were looking around the graves with Mrs. Norman. Some might see it as an invasion of privacy and I specifically asked you not to dig into people's lives."

Ruby stiffened. "My mistake then, as I was under the impression that I had a choice in the matter."

"Choices that harm others should not be utilized," he snarled. "I was very clear that I didn't want you dredging up the past. Did your troublesome sister put you up to it?"

She wanted to ask him who he thought he was, but it was obvious he considered himself judge and jury over everyone he met. "I assume you mean Violet, and you would be wrong. Surely you can appreciate that I am a grown woman with my own thoughts."

He pursed his lips for a moment. "You have always been a level-headed person. Why are you now so invested in upsetting the town?"

"That's never been my intention," Ruby protested. "There are questions that need to be answered and if you refuse to answer them, then I must seek the answers elsewhere."

"The only thing you must do, is let the dead rest in peace," he insisted.

"I would—if I knew for a fact that Meredith Denton was dead."

His face pinched. "She is dead."

Something in the way he said this sounded like more of a wish than a statement.

"Then you should have no issue with showing me her grave."

He looked away.

"I can understand that the books might not be up to date, but you can at least show me the death certificate," Ruby pressed.

He clasped his hands in front of him. "The church no longer holds death certificates."

She nodded. "Then surely Edgar must have it."

He leaned forward menacingly. "Meredith would not thank you for dragging up her—history."

His breathe fanned her face and it was all she could do not to flinch as her heart seemed to stop. "So, she is alive?"

He paused for a couple of seconds that seemed much longer. "If I take you to her, will you leave the matter there?"

"If everything is as it should be, then, yes. I'll walk away and you'll never hear from me about this again."

His eyes brightened slightly. "I have your word?"

Ruby nodded, her stomach churning with excitement at finally getting the answers she needed. She had no idea why it mattered so much to resolve a stranger's troubles but knew she would have no peace if she didn't.

He glanced at the large clock on the wall. "Are you free now?"

"I'm just closing. Give me five minutes?"

"I will wait in the parking lot at the back of the library." He glanced down at Bob. "Leave the dog, they frighten her and it's not far." He swept out the front door before she could reply and it closed behind him with a bang.

Bob whined.

"It's okay, he's gone now. I'm sorry, but you'll have to wait here, boy. I'll be as quick as I can."

The dog whined again and Ruby pulled a treat from the top drawer of her desk and gave him a good scratch before locking the front door. The treat lay on the floor at his feet and they stared at each other for a moment.

"I have to go, buddy. Don't worry."

Unsure if this was said for his benefit or hers, Ruby collected her phone and coat from her office, then went out the back door and locked that too. The minister stood beside an old van. She noted he could have walked here, so he must have been on his way home from elsewhere. He opened the passenger door and helped her up onto the seat like a gentleman. A few feet away George watched from behind a small shrub and a chill ran along her spine. The pets were ridiculously intuitive, but this was silly she told herself.

Half-turning to put on her seat belt, a hand suddenly closed over her mouth. A cloth was pressed over her nose and Ruby gasped. Stupidly this made her suck in the cloth and whatever it was doused in. She struggled. The hand held fast. Her limbs became heavy. The sweet taste coated the inside of her mouth and her nose. Unwillingly her body slid down the seat and she let the item in her hand slip. The last thing she heard was the click of the seat belt as her eyelids flickered.

Once. Twice.

Chapter Twenty-Four

Blackness hid the world and Ruby fought without conscious thought to find light.

"Open your eyes." The command came sharply from a distance.

She ran a dry tongue over her drier lips and the movement made her gag as her stomach roiled. She forced her lids to part. The narrow gap allowed her to see the minister standing shoulder to shoulder with Edgar Swanson and her heart sank. She'd been kidnapped and her foolishness fueled the anger at allowing it to happen when every fiber of her being had warned her against getting in the van.

Placing a hand on the floorboards under her chest, she found a little strength to push herself into a half-sitting position. At least she could see them better upright, though her vision was cloudy.

"We should be careful what we wish for," the minister said caustically.

Ruby imagined his sermons would be vitriolic. "You think I wanted to be kidnapped?" she rasped as she took in the room. It was bleak. The drapes were shut. A light above the men allowed her to see that all the walls were painted in a dark blue except for one. A small table was covered with food packages—the same ones that Alex used for his take outs.

"You were warned," Edgar pronounced it like a death sentence, though he didn't meet her gaze when she looked at him.

She swallowed hard. "Meredith, where is she?"

"Hello."

Ruby twisted around, immediately wishing she hadn't when she gagged again. A woman knelt behind her holding a piece of Pumpkin pie in one hand. The other one reached out and patted her hair.

"Pretty dolly."

Though she looked nothing like the woman from her imagination or indeed from the locket, Ruby could tell this was who she had been searching for. Her voice shook a little as she asked gently, "Are you Meredith?"

The woman clapped her hands and pie splattered over her clothes and the floor. "Talking dolly," she exclaimed taking no notice of the mess.

Her chipped nails were dirty and her clothes were thin and old-fashioned. Meredith smiled in a vacant way as she resumed touching Ruby as if she were a life-sized doll.

Ruby's heart ached as she turned back to the two men. "What happened to her?"

The men glanced at each other before Edgar drew himself up to his full height which was nearly a foot shorter than the man beside him.

"You insisted on knowing all the sad details, and now you do. Meredith has dementia. She couldn't be left to her own devices because she would wander and was found too many times miles from home. Often she was injured because she would step on sharp objects or twist an ankle. It was upsetting for everyone concerned."

Ruby took Meredith's hand and helped her stand. "So, you hid her away for her own safety?"

"That's right."

Edgar obviously lacked conviction. The minister was the one in charge here and Ruby knew she had to focus on him more.

Meredith still clutched her fingers, so Ruby pushed back tangled gray hair with her free hand and this small thing enabled her to finally see the resemblance to the picture in the locket. That wasn't all she saw. A long scar running from temple to ear was exposed. It was pale, therefore an old injury, but a bad one.

"What happened here?" she asked softly.

Meredith let her hand go and mimicking the gesture, cradled Ruby's face, smiling adoringly.

"I told you. She fell and hit her head."

Ruby ignored Edgar and lightly touched the scar. Meredith recoiled. "Does it hurt here?"

Meredith nodded, then her eyes clouded and she shook her head. She put a finger to her lips. "Shhh. Don't cry. Don't cry," she moaned.

"That's enough!" Edgar hissed. "You'll traumatize her and she gets fractious when upset."

The minister took a step forward and pulled Meredith away. The woman pursed her lips but didn't fuss when the minister hissed. "You said if you saw her we would be done with any more questions."

Ruby raked both men with a glare. "To see her and to know she is well taken care of are two completely different things."

Edgar's eyes widened. "What do you mean? We have

done the very best we could given the circumstances. You don't understand what it's been like. Unfortunately, my aunt has had mental health issues for many years and my mother couldn't deal with it. Meredith was kept in a room in the basement until my mother got sick and decided she should go to an institution."

Ruby flinched at the hatred in his voice for his mother. "So the two of you got together and hid her away instead of getting her professional care."

"We didn't have the funds for a private institution, and all the ones I looked into were horrible," Edgar told her evenly, though the words seemed to hurt him. "Mother didn't want me to be responsible for my aunt any longer. She had power of attorney for her health and finances of which Meredith had none."

He added the last hastily. Perhaps in case Ruby would think he had done all this for money. If he only knew she'd ruled that out a while ago. "So, in her way, your mother was looking out for you?" Ruby asked carefully.

He shifted uncomfortably. "Not at all. I was the one who made sure Meredith had what she needed. Especially, when my mother became infirm after a stroke. I was the only one she would allow to see her that way and she didn't like my attention being divided. I went to Ambrose and asked him to help me. He suggested the cottage."

The minister frowned. "Agatha was a hard woman and had treated Meredith poorly for years. I had always wanted to help her, but Agatha wouldn't allow me near the place. She threatened me more than once."

He didn't elaborate, but then he didn't need to. Ruby paced the room, searching their words for some sense. There were at least two flaws in their explanations and reasoning. "If this really is the truth, why did you kidnap me?"

"Kidnap?" Edgar shook his head in denial. "You keep saying that..."

She tapped her foot, much to Meredith's delight. The woman copied her with a grin. Ruby wanted to talk to her, but she had to deal with these delusional men first. "That's what I'd call it, and I'm sure the police will think the same thing. I was drugged and brought here against my will—how does that sound to you Edgar?"

"The police?" The minister yelled. "We had your word."

"My word was given sincerely—before the kidnapping. Before seeing Meredith."

"I'm very sorry to hear that."

Ambrose spoke so softly, Ruby hoped she had imagined the threat.

"What do you mean?" Edgar's shock oddly clarified her situation. He was nothing but a pawn and was only now getting the significance of what they had done. He was a co-conspirator, regardless of whether he had known where it would all lead.

"He means to kill me," Ruby said flatly.

Edgar flinched and drew back. "No, he doesn't. That's not what this meeting is about. We just want you to leave us alone and we thought once you saw Meredith and her issues, you would do that."

Ruby shook her head at his naivety. "Think about it, Edgar. A meeting is when two parties get together willingly to discuss a matter. They agree or disagree, then all parties go home. The minister doesn't want me to leave here, knowing what I do."

"She'll make things up. We can't trust her," the minister growled at Edgar.

"The question is, do you trust a man of the cloth who is supposed to be good and just? A man who kidnaps women? Go ahead, ask him what he intends to do with me."

Edgar turned, his voice full of desperation. "Tell her that isn't your intention."

"No one can know about Meredith," the minister said evenly. "They'll take her away from me—from us."

That small slip was enough for Ruby. As soon as she saw that scar, she knew that the minister had done far more than hide a mentally unhinged woman from the world. "You did that to her, didn't you?" she demanded.

Edgar stared at the minister in horror, as if he was seeing him in another light. "It was an accident. She fell. Isn't that right, Ambrose?"

"That's exactly what happened," the minister yelled. "Don't let this woman poison your mind. We have done the very best we could for Meredith and we won't be undone by a librarian's interference."

Edgar wrung his hands. "All my life, I have taken care of Meredith in one way or another. Like you, I wanted people to leave us alone, Ambrose, but now I see it is impossible to stop the truth coming out." He took a step forward. "I will not let you kill this young woman."

Ruby watched them closely. The minister wasn't a young man. Since Edgar was born in 1961 and was age 62, then the minister had to be about seventy. But Edgar was overweight and timid. The minister was lean and wiry. He was also angry and looked to be backing himself if it came to a physical altercation.

"I don't think you will stop me, Edgar," he growled.

"Not if you don't want to be held accountable for hiding Meredith all this time."

Edgar stilled. "We are both accountable."

"It is your name on the deed of this cottage. Not mine. And there were all those years in your mother's basement when you did nothing."

The sanctimonious look on the minister's face infuriated Ruby, and it seemed by his furious expression that Edgar wasn't far behind. While it was likely from the shock of the minister's admission, Ruby needed him to be completely on her side and reject Ambrose's plans.

"You wanted this all along didn't you? You brought me here to force Edgar into doing something he would never have considered, and thereby making him as guilty as you for Meredith's situation. I daresay you expect him to do the deed, leaving your false innocence intact should this get out —which I can assure you it will."

Her accusation wasn't perhaps her best plan as it tipped the minister over the edge.

Specks of spittle landed on Edgar's cheek.

"I will not go to prison. Meredith would die without me. If you're thinking of choosing this upstart over our Meredith, after all we've been though protecting her, then you are not the man I thought you were."

Edgar swallowed hard, already wavering. "You know I've always tried to do right by Meredith, but maybe it's time we got help. I know she gets lonely by how desperately she clings to me if I leave and I need to work."

The woman in question was still clutching the minister's arm, staring vacantly around the room. She smiled at Ruby whenever their eyes met and Ruby smiled back though it was forced. Naturally she was scared about the outcome, but she was so angry with these men who had made decisions they seriously thought were in Meredith's best interest.

She pointed at each of them. "Do you honestly believe she has any quality of life? Does she get out into the fresh air, or does she live in these dirty and dilapidated four walls, waiting for a few spare minutes of your time?"

"Meredith is happy every time she sees one of us," the minister yelled. "We are all she needs!"

Meredith flinched and leaned away, but he didn't let her go.

"And when you're not here? What then? I see no books and aren't they what she loved? Although the light in here is too poor to read anyway."

Edgar nodded sadly. "There didn't seem to be much point as she can't focus on anything except her doll for very long. She used to love to play the piano, but we couldn't get one in here without movers and we didn't want anyone to know where she was."

Ruby wanted to scream at his stupidity and weakness. "Never mind a piano or the fact that just holding a book you love can evoke good memories. What about the basics? She's dirty and the place is cold, Edgar. What happens when she gets sick?"

"We'll give her medicine," he muttered defensively.

"Without seeing a doctor? Even if your mother was the one who kept her locked up at the estate, she was looked after better than this, wasn't she? Somebody made decent food for her and washed her clothes and bathed her. I don't understand how you can think living this way is acceptable for a person you love."

"Shut up!" the minister roared again, causing Meredith to cower. "Edgar, do not listen to her. She's ruining everything."

Ruby took another step closer and thumped her chest. "I'm not the one who injured this poor woman. I'm not the one who kidnapped her and hid her in a run-down cottage with bars on the windows. I mean, that wound must have been bad, did you even get her checked out? Perhaps her head injury could have been reversed and it's not dementia at all."

Edgar's mouth dropped open.

"What if there was still a chance you could bring her back to who she was? What if she could have a better quality of life?" Ruby pressed.

The minister thrust Meredith at Edgar. The woman whimpered, but he ignored this and reached instead for Ruby.

She backed away to the corner of the room. "Don't you dare touch me!"

"You've said and done enough," he growled. "This needs to end now."

He was faster than she would have given him credit for. His bony hands clutched her wrist and squeezed hard.

"Ouch! Let me go."

"Please, Ambrose. Don't hurt her."

"She lied and you can see she intends to ruin us, Edgar. It's too late for mercy."

"I'd say that was ironic for a man of the cloth," Ruby blustered while her heart and mind raced. How was she to get out of this mess alive to help poor Meredith?

Ambrose shrugged. "I have worked tirelessly for the community which ensures that no one would believe your accusations, but I won't run the risk. Sometimes hard decisions must be made," he told her casually as if that made killing her completely understandable.

He wasn't right in the head, Ruby acknowledged to

herself. There was no point in wasting time trying to talk him around the way she might other people. People who didn't intend to kill her.

He still had her wrist and was probably stronger than her if it came to hand-to-hand combat, but she was small and fast. When you had two older, taller, opinionated sisters, she'd needed an edge and this was it.

This skill she'd developed was something she only used when the need was desperate, and right now she was every kind of desperate.

Could it work here? She didn't know, but this might be the only chance she had.

Chapter Twenty-Five

Ruby bent her wrist forcing his backward and thrust herself into his midriff catching him off balance. Using the leverage she pulled him over her body. The weight bowed her but she continued the move until he landed flat on his back.

Meredith shrieked and prostrated herself on top of the minister as if she might protect him.

"I'm sorry, Meredith," Ruby said, but the woman couldn't hear her amidst her wails.

Ambrose attempted to get to his feet while Meredith refused to budge and Ruby was torn between comforting her and escaping.

Suddenly Edgar pushed her away. "Go!" He thrust a large key into her palm. "Hurry!"

"What about you?"

His gave a quick sad smile. "I made Meredith a promise. I'll stay and face the consequences of my actions."

"Traitor!" The minister roared and pulled a gun from his robe.

Ruby launched herself at Edgar just as the gun went off. Her face scraped across the wood floor and her cheek was instantly sticky with blood, but there was no pain.

A loud bang came from behind the locked door and then it burst open.

"Nate! Alex!" Ruby had never been happier to see either of them.

The two men, one big and the other gigantic almost got stuck in the doorway. It might have been funny, if she wasn't still trying to tamp down her fear of being shot. Then Alex was at her side and hauling a moaning Edgar from her.

"Please be gentle," she called as he dropped the man against the wall a couple feet away.

Alex made a disparaging sound but did as she asked and righted Edgar so he was sitting up. That's when they saw the wound on his arm.

Meanwhile, Nate was kneeling on the minister's back and already had one cuff on him. Next to them—Meredith sat holding the gun. She turned it this way and that.

"Nate," Ruby called as loudly as she dared without startling the poor woman. "Meredith has the gun."

He turned, just as she raised it to her head.

Ruby was fast, but Nate flew across the room to knock the gun from her hand first. Meredith blinked several times before she smiled as if it had been some kind of joke.

Ruby let out a loud breath. "Call an ambulance, Alex."

He was beside her once more, his eyes still wary as he studied both men, but he pulled out his phone.

Nate handed Meredith his notebook and pen and got her to sit down and draw before turning back to the minister who was pleading his case in more reasonable tones than he had used with her.

"He kidnapped me and Meredith," she interrupted.

"That's not true. It was Edgar," he insisted.

Edgar shook his head, his eyes never leaving Meredith who was drawing quietly and singing in a childish way about a butterfly.

Ruby crept across the room and touched Meredith's head. When the woman didn't fuss, she ran her fingers up the scar and felt an indentation hidden by her hair. Speaking softly she addressed Nate.

"She has a wound on her head which I think a doctor might find attributed to her problems. A wound the minister admitted to causing. He wanted to keep Meredith to himself and not let her tell the story of her babies and that he was the father."

Ambrose shook his head. "You're just guessing."

Ignoring the minister, Nate waited patiently for her to continue.

"There is a little of that," she admitted to him, "but it's a calculated guess. All the time she has been secreted away, he never took her to a doctor, so all his talk about caring for her is just that. He didn't love her at all."

"You stupid girl! I loved her more than is right. I found her in the middle of the countryside, running away from her family who had kept her locked away. I hadn't seen her for years and she was distraught and scared."

Ruby turned away from him and addressed Edgar. "Was she initially locked away by your mother after she lost the babies?"

He nodded, holding his injured arm where Alex had wrapped a piece of his shirt around the bullet wound. "We tried to keep her close to the house, but she would wander and in the end mother insisted she needed constant watching. Then mother had her first stroke and I had the two of them to care for as well as my work running the estate. Mother insisted on the locked room and I couldn't see another option. I tried to make the room nice. I painted a picture of the hills beyond her walls, and I swapped the books whenever she asked, but Meredith hated being in that room. She didn't understand what was wrong with her. She was often like a caged lion." Fat tears rolled down his cheeks. "I did what I could but I should have done more."

Ruby remembered that patch in the locked room of the estate. It must have been a similar picture and painted over before Edgar sold the place. "Yes, you should have. And you shouldn't have listened to this self-centered maniac after your mother died."

Alex's eyes widened. He wasn't used to her being mean and it must be quite a shock, she decided. Still, it was better he knew now about the temper she rarely let lose but was equal to Violet's when she did. These words had to be said and there was no better time to hear the truth. With Edgar repentant and not under the minister's thumb any longer, she would drag all the gory details out of them—for Meredith's sake.

"I am not self-centered! I gave up my life for her," Ambrose was explaining.

"I see no evidence of you giving up anything when you have a house attached to the church with all the modern comforts Meredith certainly doesn't have here! And how could you have hurt her like that?" Ruby pointed disdainfully at the scar. Still slightly pink after all this time. "She was the mother of your children."

He flinched, but his shame was fleeting, even though he didn't deny that the babies were his. "You don't understand.

She was crazed after the loss of her children and Agatha keeping her locked away because of it didn't help. She had forgotten her babies were dead and she wanted to find them and take them as far from Cozy Hollow as possible. I couldn't let her leave in that state again. What would have become of an unwed mother who wasn't worldly in any way?"

Nate stared at her and she nodded. Perhaps the minister was confused, but it sounded like he was talking about two separate incidents and Ruby's suspicions grew.

"Oh, I understand perfectly well that you couldn't allow that to happen. People would have found out what a despicable person you are. If she left, you wouldn't have her under your control and you didn't want your relationship exposed for what it was. I should imagine you were horrified by the situation. What if she mentioned your name and the church found out how you had coerced an innocent teenager to be your lover and that she had born you children out of wedlock?"

"There was no coercion. Still, things were different back then," Ambrose acknowledged reluctantly.

"You had choices and by doing what you did, you left Meredith with none. Her sister kept her locked away and she escaped. Only to end up your prisoner instead."

"Hardly a prisoner." He pointed at the childlike woman on the cold floor. "You see her. She could never take care of herself."

"You appear to be ignorant of what the word care means. It seems to me, that when Meredith told you what she intended, you fought with her and you hit her—the woman you supposedly loved."

He was pale and shaking now, but no less adamant in

his righteousness. "Edgar came to find me and tell me that she had escaped and he was worried for her safety. The two of us scoured the countryside in the rain. There is no denying that the childbirth experience affected her and she was incoherent when I found her roaming the hills looking for the babies."

"Your babies," Ruby reminded him.

He grunted. "Her mind had taken her back to that time but omitted the part about them being dead. She wouldn't listen to reason or go back home. I merely meant to shock her with a slap, but she jerked away and slipped on the wet grass." He rubbed a hand over his eyes. "She fell heavily, hitting her head on a stone. There was so much blood and she was unconscious for a long time. I carried her across the fields to the estate. After I staunched the flow and sewed the wound while she rocked and asked for the children, Agatha insisted that Meredith be locked in a room. It seemed like the only answer until Agatha died. Edgar bought this cottage and she was safe again from prying eyes."

Ruby almost gagged at his view of her being safe and the way he looked at Meredith with such sadness. Truly, if Ruby hadn't seen the state of the woman or heard most of the story by now she might have been inclined to pity him.

Only, he deserved no pity. He'd had so many options. If the church had turned their back on him or made life difficult, he could have left the ministry and married her, giving his children his name and being a family. They could have lived happily elsewhere instead of this second house of despair.

She shuddered. No one would have found out about her plight if Meredith had not previously penned those notes, and if Edgar had not given Gail the books. Had Edgar known what was hidden in them? Was he looking for a way out from the deception and lies all this time?

Ruby studied him as the siren wails drew nearer. She decided he might have, even if it wasn't a conscious thought. He loved his aunt who was more like a sister and Ambrose had used that love to make him an accomplice.

And, what about the babies?

Chapter Twenty-Six

Sam, the paramedic treated Edgar's wound which had been superficial and more of a graze. It required nothing more than cleaning and a bandage. After that, both men were taken separately to the station.

Alex and Ruby sat in the back of Nate's car holding hands. She was lost in her thoughts, and wondering if her sisters knew what had happened yet.

"We'll need your statements and then you can see your sisters, Ruby," Nate said as he drove.

She smiled at how well he knew her. Oddly, that in turn made her stomach twist. They understood so much more about Meredith's plight, but Ruby needed to hear the whole story and only one person could deliver that with honesty. She leaned close to the grill between them. "What will happen to Meredith?"

Nate's eyes met hers in the mirror. "The ambulance will take her to the hospital in Destiny for assessment. After that, I can't say."

"It seems a shame that she and Edgar will be separated for what I can only imagine will be a very long time."

"He did aide the minister," Nate said gruffly.

"I know, but I think he initially did it for the right reasons. He seemed to have been coerced by someone he thought had all the answers. I don't think he has the ability to make his own decisions and for him it was the lesser of two evils. I suspect he didn't know how to undo the situation his mother had forced on him."

"You are right," Alex stated flatly. "And so is Nate. It was evil what they did—both of them."

Ruby placed her other hand on his and squeezed. "I know it looks that way, but sometimes things are more convoluted than we think because of circumstances. Sometimes people do terrible things because they believe there are no other options."

Alex stared at her for a few moments before nodding and she knew that he understood what she meant. She also appreciated that he wasn't in total agreement with her. Leaning forward again she asked the impossible of a friend and almost family member. "Would you let me hear Edgar's side of the story?"

Nate blew out a whistling breath. "I'm sorry Ruby, I can't allow that. Questioning isn't exactly a spectator sport, no matter what you see on television."

She sighed. "I really want to know the whole thing, and more than that, I think Edgar would tell me."

"You mean he'd tell the truth for once, because you're Ruby Finch?"

Her cheeks flamed while Nate shot her another look in the rear-view mirror. He was right, but it wasn't out of any self-importance that she believed it to be true. People told her things and asked her advice. It was a thing, and Nate knew this. Heck, the minister had practically spilled everything because of her pushing, right in that run-down cottage.

The silence grew and just when she had given up hope he blew out another breath.

"Perhaps I could wrangle something, by letting you spend some time with him while we interview the minister —if Edgar is agreeable and I have a spare deputy to stand guard."

"I'm sure he wants to get it off his chest," Ruby told him, a shiver of anticipation washing over her.

"If anyone can get the truth from a man it would be Ruby," Alex said proudly.

"I don't doubt it," Nate muttered and pulled around the back of the station and into the parking lot.

"I will stand guard as well," Alex said casually. "We don't know this weak man well, but weak men can do bad things when cornered."

"Yeah, that's absolutely not happening. You can watch from another room close by and that's my best offer to both of you," Nate growled. "At the first sign of trouble you are out of there, understand?"

When they nodded a little sheepishly, he let them out and showed them inside to a sparsely furnished room. A metal table was attached to the floor with large bolts and two metal chairs sat on either side of it. Ruby had never been in the cells and she wondered how many rooms like this were in the small station and if they were ever full.

"Ruby, please take a seat and remain seated until you're done, or I come to get you. Alex, you follow me. You'll be right next door, but you better stay there or I will not be happy."

Alex took a step closer to Ruby. "I must make sure she is safe."

"It has a two-way mirror and I won't lock the door, but I mean what I say about staying there, otherwise you'll have to go now."

"I'll be fine," Ruby assured Alex. "Edgar is not a violent man and even if you were able to stay in the room, he'd hardly say anything in front of you which would defeat the purpose."

White lines showed around Alex's mouth, but he followed Nate. She heard another door open and close and made a face at the glass to her left. She couldn't be sure, but she thought she heard his deep chuckle.

It was several minutes before Officer Glasson led Edgar into the room. Cradling his arm in a sling he looked very sorry for himself and a little indignant when he was cuffed to the desk by his good arm. Officer Glasson left the room and she heard the door being locked.

Ruby smiled encouragingly. "Hi Edgar. Do you mind if we chat for a bit?"

Edgar slumped forward. "Chat? I don't understand why you are here. You're not the police."

She nodded. "That's true, but I have desperately wanted to help Meredith ever since I found the notes she hid in her favorite books and long before I realized she was the one who had written them. Now that she is free, I'd really like to know her story. And yours if you don't mind sharing?"

He simply stared at her as if he didn't know what to do.

"I know this seems odd and that you're worried about Meredith. You don't have to talk to me, but it will be a while before we hear how she is and you can rest assured that she is safe and being taken care of."

He rubbed the back of his head with his good arm. "I know it's for the best that she is being attended to properly, only Meredith will be scared at being in a new place with strangers."

"The staff at Destiny hospital are great. They'll do some tests to see how best they can help her. Wouldn't that be good if they could make things a little better than they have been?"

Eyes misting, Edgar nodded then gave a heavy sigh. "Meredith made everything easier to cope with. If it wasn't for her, I would have run away from home at a young age and never come back. We were more like siblings than aunt and nephew and though we were unhappy with our circumstances we had each other. That helped more than you can know."

"You loved each other," Ruby stated simply.

Chapter Twenty-Seven

He offered her a watery smile. "I felt so lucky to have one person in my life who did love me. My mother didn't care for boys. She wanted a daughter, and with Meredith living with us she had one."

Ruby tutted. "I'm sure Agatha must have loved you."

"Not even a little." He laughed bitterly. "I'm not making it up to get your sympathy. My mother told me often enough that I was a grubby beast and that I was stupid like my father—like all men."

This was so sad that Ruby felt her throat close a little. "Didn't your parents get along?"

"They detested each other." He grimaced. "I heard my mother talking to Meredith one day about arranged marriages and that my aunt should behave if she didn't want to suffer the same fate. That was the day I heard how much she loathed being married to my father. Not that I needed it spelled out. They couldn't be in the same room as each other without sarcasm bouncing off the walls. I'm sure that looking like my father didn't help."

"Your father died when you were a preteen, didn't he?"

He nodded. "It was a hunting accident. He wasn't exactly warm either, but he at least asked me how I was from time to time and taught me how to ride. Father was disappointed that I didn't like hunting." He stared at the far wall and sighed. "It seems I disappoint everyone."

"Did he manage the estate?"

"Yes, but he never interfered with anything to do with the house, including my upbringing. I think he was scared of my mother who had a caustic tongue."

Ruby couldn't help being affected by his words which held pain and sorrow as he continued.

"One day I heard her speaking to Meredith about miscarriages and how my mother had many, which I guess was what made her so bitter. She also said that although my birth was difficult, she had at least provided an heir but she really wanted a daughter."

"I'm so sorry, Edgar. These things must have been hard to hear, especially as a child."

He looked away. "In some ways it was a relief to finally know why she disliked me so much. I tried so hard to be an obedient child, but she couldn't look at me with anything but disdain."

Ruby swallowed hard, imagining the young boy living in such a hostile environment. An environment that clearly hadn't gotten better through the years and would have been a lot worse without Meredith. "Tell me about growing up with your aunt."

He smiled and his face lit up. "Everyone adored her. My mother called her a simple fool, but she loved her too. There was a sixteen-year difference in their ages, but my mother had taken care of her from birth until she married and treated Meredith like the daughter she craved." The smile lifted to be replaced once more with bitterness. "Until Meredith's beauty began to be acknowledged. After that, Meredith was kept close to home. She was a teenager and full of life when the minister came to town."

"So she was allowed out then?"

He gave a small half-smile. "We were always a private family. Mother didn't encourage visitors, but we were involved in the local community in a small way. My father more so, with the farm and workers. After he passed away was about the time we all kept more to ourselves and Meredith became home-schooled. I didn't mind so much for me. I was a shy boy and the farm held enough of my attention."

"But Meredith wasn't like that?"

The smile widened. "Not at all. She craved company and made lots of friends. Even though they weren't allowed to come to the house."

"Yet she was cut off just like that? With no fuss?"

"She argued repeatedly with my mother, but there was no changing her mind." He shrugged. "Maybe that's why Meredith was allowed to spend time with the minister."

"As long as you were with her?" Ruby prompted.

"I was used intentionally or not, as their chaperone," he agreed. "At first my mother didn't notice how Ambrose looked at my aunt. She considered a minister would be a good influence and it created a diversion from Meredith missing her friends too much as some of them were in the choir. I don't know whose idea it was, but after a while we began taking Meredith for walks. She loved to talk about nature, painting, and music and he seemed to have a lot to say about them."

Edgar's face darkened and he was silent for a minute.

"After several of these outings, Meredith insisted that they be left alone to chat. Though I knew mother wouldn't like it, I was happy roaming the woods and not having to listen to them talking about things that held no interest for me."

"Did you notice the attraction between them right away?"

He nodded. "From that first meeting, Meredith changed. She was fifteen when they met. She giggled when he spoke to her and was always touching her hair. Having already been kept at home as company for my mother, Meredith had been sheltered and wasn't used to adult male attention. She wasn't worldly in any respect and Ambrose had traveled extensively. He was twenty-three when he came to the church as a minister. I guess she was fascinated by him."

Ruby's heart hurt for Meredith. It sounded as if the girl had never had a say over her life. Perhaps safe from a forced marriage, she had almost certainly wanted more than Agatha could give her. Her sister wasn't a good role model, but she'd clearly had her own demons. They all had issues, but when Ruby thought of Ambrose, she still couldn't feel any sympathy. He had taken advantage of Meredith's situation and his to get what he wanted.

"Except for those walks, it must have been tricky for them to find time alone. He was a minister after all and had duties to perform outside of the choir and Sunday services."

Anger flashed across Edgar's features for a moment before he continued the story.

"After a few months, he encouraged my mother to allow Meredith to join the choir. It meant that she would be with him for a couple of hours around other people and then he would walk her home. That's when the real secret liaison began. That walk home which should have taken twenty minutes often took an hour." His face turned red to his ears. "I had daily tasks to do around the farm by then and was sent to meet them. Often I had to wait for them to turn up and I can only assume my mother thought we were together the whole time. I saw him kiss her one day and was shocked and wanted to tell someone, but she was so happy. Seeing her laugh made me think it would be cruel to stop her from having fun and she always spoke about her time with him as if it were innocent." He shook his head. "It was impossible to think ill of her."

Ruby could see his guilt burdened him and that he was experiencing some relief at getting it off his chest. In many ways he was also a simple man and like Meredith he had been brow-beaten by the people around him to conform and not rock the boat. While he wasn't innocent, he was also a victim. "What happened then?" she asked gently.

"Meredith started to come out of her shell and her friends from school asked where she had been and why she didn't attend any parties. She let it slip that my mother was very strict. When the gossip got back to my mother, that and all the renewed attention on Meredith made her furious. She insisted Meredith quit the choir and since no one went against my mother that was that. Like me, Meredith wasn't strong enough to stand up for herself and she descended into despair which only made my mother angrier. Mother wanted the old Meredith back. Someone she could vent to who would listen and didn't argue about fairness. Someone who mother didn't have to pretend to that she was a happy lady of the manor. I was at best, second choice in that respect when mother had no one else.

Ruby could see that Edgar had found ways to justify his

behavior to himself to make it more palatable. While it was clear that he had been unhappy with his aunt's relationship with Ambrose, he had allowed it and in fact helped make it possible. This must have weighed heavily on his shoulders and it confused Ruby because of Meredith's current predicament and how it came to be.

"Why did you help Ambrose by keeping her hidden?" she asked.

"It was for Meredith not him!" The words hissed out of him. "You can't imagine how distraught she was and it got worse the longer she was confined. Of course by the time things came to a head, she must have realized that she was pregnant. She begged me to take her to him. On a rare occasion when mother went to town I relented. They met near the stream at the back of our land and she told him she was having his child and that she had to get away from my mother before the truth was obvious."

Ruby blinked, picturing the scene, and not liking what she imagined was about to follow. "How did he react to the news?"

"Ambrose was horrified. I don't think he had given the possibility of a pregnancy any thought and put the blame on her. He told Meredith he could never leave his parish and she had to deal with this on her own as the shame would ruin him. He said that she could never tell anyone that he was the father of her baby. She cried and pleaded with him for a long time, but he refused to bend or find a way out of the mess."

"And there was no talk of marriage?"

"There was, but not from him. I was waiting a few yards away and it broke my heart to hear Meredith's anguish, so I joined them. I told him he must marry her, but he looked

184

confused and said that wasn't possible and he had to get back to the church. By this time Meredith was hysterical. She said she would kill herself and his child. That shocked him, but not in a good way. He said that was an evil thing to consider, let alone do."

"Wow. I bet that didn't help Meredith."

He sighed. "I couldn't bear to see her this way and I told Ambrose that she wasn't the evil one here and when it got out that he had not only gotten her pregnant, but forsaken her, he would be run out of the village. He was appalled, but he could see that it wouldn't take long for everyone to put two and two together. Eventually, Ambrose told her to give him time to work things out and he made me bring her home."

Ruby's mind was spinning. "You took her home? To your mother?"

"I didn't know what else to do. It was clear that he didn't want her in that condition, but I still had hope that he would find a way to work things out for the best once he considered his options and came to his senses."

"Which never happened," Ruby said dryly. "It must have been hard keeping her secret."

"You have no idea." Edgar sighed. "We snuck back into the house and Meredith managed to clean herself up before mother saw her. For the next month Meredith carried on as normal, though it was obvious to me that she was heartsick and dwelling on her predicament. I promised her repeatedly that I would take care of her. I guess after a while she didn't believe me."

His sadness was real and Ruby's heart was sore for him. "Or perhaps she didn't want to put you in the position of going against your mother."

185

He smiled wanly at that. "Meredith would have considered that."

"I know it's a terrible thing to think about after everything that happened today, but up on the hill behind the house is obviously where the babies were buried—how did they die?" Ruby asked softly.

Chapter Twenty-Eight

He paled, and his voice shook, yet to his credit, Edgar seemed determined to get all the story out once and for all. "Several weeks following their meeting, Meredith ran away one night. She hadn't seen the minister or heard from him and the pregnancy was starting to show. The only reason mother hadn't noticed was that she was ill and had taken to her bed. We were both scared of my mother's reaction when she did find out and Meredith couldn't bear anticipating that happening at any moment."

"Where did she run to?

"No one will ever know what her intention was that night," he told her, his voice etched in sadness. "I began the search for her not long after dawn. I couldn't sleep and when I went down the hall to her room, she was gone along with her coat, shoes, and some of her clothes. It took me all day to find her and it was too late by the time I did."

He swallowed hard and it took a moment for him to continue. "In the forest that runs along the top of the ridge, I found her shoe wedged under a tree trunk. I believe she tripped on the trunk and fell into a ravine. The fall must have induced labor and she had twisted an ankle, so she couldn't climb out, though there was evidence of her attempting to pull herself up the slippery walls. She lay in a couple of inches of water for hours and when the babies came too soon and with no help, they died." He gasped and tears slid down his cheeks.

"When I found her, Meredith still lay in the mud and damp, cradling the babies in her arms wrapped in her shawl. They were all covered in blood and she refused to let them go long enough for us to climb out. I had to leave her there while I got help. All those hours alone with them—I think that's when she began to unravel."

"So your mother did know about the babies?" Ruby asked gently.

His hands balled into fists. "I couldn't keep it from her. Even if I had been able to take them from her and bury them, Meredith would not stop moaning about her little girls. Our stable hand and I brought a large hay barrow to the ravine and that's how we took them back to the house." He gulped several times. "A doctor came and sedated Meredith and from that day she was never the same. Some days she knew they were dead and other days she wanted to search for them. Mother even allowed me to put up the crosses and show them to Meredith, but it didn't help. We never had a funeral and there are no records they had existed."

Ruby dabbed at her cheeks with her sleeve. "Everyone pretended it never happened."

He nodded. "At mother's instruction. Only the family and the stable hand knew about it and he was paid hand-somely to keep his mouth shut. A year later he took his money and left and we never saw him again. The doctor was bound by his oath and he too has moved on."

This sounded suspicious, but Ruby had something more urgent she wanted clarified. "And that's when your mother locked Meredith up?"

His eyes glittered with tears. "I hated it. She needed help, but we weren't the kind of family that sought it. At least that is what I had been taught. We must keep up appearances at all costs and that meant hiding Meredith's indiscretion and her mental health."

Ruby gaped. "And the minister got off scot-free?"

"Not long after he got a job at a church in Destiny. Years later I heard that he was engaged, but the wedding was called off. Then one day he contacted me and asked about Meredith. I guess he really wanted to know about the babies."

"That seems off when he was so scared of being found out and stripped of his livelihood."

"I thought that way too and I told him that there were no babies and he should leave us alone." Edgar rubbed his face roughly with his palms. "If he had stayed away, if I had ignored him, she wouldn't be in the state she is now."

Ruby couldn't agree more, but she didn't want to stop his flow so she ignored this. "What did he do?"

"He kept harassing me and went on and on about how he had changed and that Meredith being shut away was cruel."

Ruby could have raged about versions of cruelty, but she had already decided that Edgar had done his best given the circumstances. He was not a man to buck the system, or someone who wielded confidence. He was a pushover and Ambrose knew this already and used it to get what he wanted—Meredith. When she was no longer pregnant, he wanted her again as if she were a piece of property to own and manage.

The bitterness was difficult to hide. "So he encouraged you to get Meredith to run away again, but this time he had a plan."

"I don't know what medication my mother gave her, or how regularly Meredith took it, but sometimes she was quite lucid and we spoke as if none of the bad things had happened. When Ambrose came to me with his plan a few years ago it sounded feasible. He had his eye on an old cottage and told me if I bought it, Meredith would be happy there away from prying eyes and could live her life the way she chose. When I mentioned his suggestion, Meredith lit up and a spark came back. It gave me hope and made me think it was a good idea. If things had been different, maybe that would have been enough for her."

Though it disturbed her on many levels, Ruby could see that this had some merit. "What happened when they met?"

He rubbed his face again. "I think you can imagine. Seeing him brought back memories of the babies and that night in the rain. She accused him of leaving them and her to die, as punishment because she had threatened it. I didn't even know she remembered that conversation. She began hitting him and even picked up a piece of wood. He pushed her away and she fell backward and hit her head on an old stone wall. The wound was deep and she blacked out for some time. When she came to, she was confused, but docile. We carried her to the cottage and he fixed the wound."

"So he didn't seek any medical help?"

"He said he had training and it would be fine."

Edgar had failed Meredith again and Ruby couldn't

help the shortness of her next question. "But it wasn't fine, was it?"

He sagged again. "Meredith had see-sawing emotions. One moment she was meek as a lamb and the next she was screeching and violent. Eventually, I brought some of the pills my mother still had. When they ran out, Ambrose got some from elsewhere and they made her more even tempered."

"Why did the police not look for her?" Ruby managed through gritted teeth as she pictured the once more drugged up Meredith.

"My mother said she had gone to live with cousins in Portland so there would be no inquiry."

"But why would she do that when a search would have found her?"

"Because by now my mother had stopped being interested in Meredith. She decided that if her sister didn't want to do as she was told, and was so desperate to go, then that was best for all of us."

"Did your mother ever know of your involvement in it all?"

"If she did she never let on and certainly never discussed the babies from the day they were buried. It was as if it never happened and my mother insisted she had done all she could for her ungrateful sister."

The story was too tragic for words and Ruby was exhausted by the roller coaster of emotions hearing it had evoked. Edgar didn't look any better than she felt.

He rubbed his face once more. "I suppose I'll have to tell this again to the police."

Ruby nodded. "They'll want to hear it first-hand. Thank you for sharing the story with me though. I know it was difficult and I'm sorry for the pain I've caused you by digging all this up."

He waved a hand sadly. "I should thank you. At least now it's all out in the open and Meredith will finally get the help she needs. Also, I no longer have to keep my family's secrets and that is a weight off my shoulders. I thought a lot about what you said that day. That no one cared about them. I said I did, yet I know I was stupid to let everyone manipulate me because the truth isn't the worst thing that can happen, is it? I wish I had been stronger." His voice faded away. "For Meredith."

Though she wished for that too, what was done wouldn't be undone by wishes or anything else. Ruby put a hand over his. "Only one person is responsible for the mess of Meredith's life, and that is Ambrose."

He glanced up hopefully, then his face fell. "If only I could believe that."

"Edgar, can I ask one more question?"

He nodded.

"Who did Meredith write the notes for?"

Tears spilled down his cheeks. "You know about the notes? I had forgotten about them. I don't know who Meredith thought would find them except me. Other than mother, I was the only one who used the library and I thought there were only the couple I found. If I could turn back time, I would have run away with her."

He broke down and Ruby left him to his sorrow, wishing he could do just that and knowing he would live with his guilt and shame for the rest of his life.

Epilogue

In the diner, Alex lay a platter of deep-fried chicken, salad, and fries on the table. He took a seat next to Ruby and draped an arm loosely around her shoulders, kissing the top of her head. "I am glad that your case is solved."

Nate coughed. "You mean *the* case—not Ruby's case."

Alex raised an eyebrow. "There was no case until Ruby discovered it and she did solve it."

"Well, yes," Nate reluctantly agreed.

"Still," Alex conceded graciously. "I am grateful you helped save her."

"Gee, thanks for that. Although, you must admit that it was George who really saved her."

"George?" Ruby looked outside to where the tabby perched peering in at them accusingly.

"George made a din at the diner and got Boris riled up. They wouldn't stop fussing until Alex followed them to the library," Nate explained.

"I found Bob locked inside, but you were gone. Then I found your phone in the parking lot, so I phoned Nate and he came right away. We asked George where you were and he led us to the cottage," Alex said matter-of-factly.

Nate snorted. "That was a leap of faith as you can imagine. Then again, anything to do with this family takes a bit of..."

"Open-mindedness." Scarlett nudged him.

Ruby laughed. "It doesn't matter who solved the case, because we all helped make it right. Although, perhaps a little spoiling wouldn't hurt our furry friends."

"Here, here," Aunt Olivia said and clinked her glass of water against Ruby's. "I want to add that your mother would have been so proud of you girls. The way you used your talents to find Meredith against all odds was amazing."

Ruby's heart filled with warmth. "Let's hope Meredith will be taken care of properly now and that she won't miss Edgar too much."

Violet made a disgusted noise. "What gets me is why the minister never move on properly. He had every opportunity once he'd walked away the first time."

"It was all about control," Scarlett stated sadly. "It sounds like he couldn't have that with any woman—except one who was already broken. Fortunately, the minister's 'love' is not the norm."

Ruby nodded. "I did some digging into the minister's engagement and found out she was a teacher. Jerome had done his training with someone who worked with the woman and she was happy to share what she knew. Apparently, he was overly possessive and it was the woman who called off the wedding. Personally, I think she had a narrow escape."

"I didn't know you'd been talking to Jerome," Violet said stiffly.

"He does come to the library most weeks," Ruby

reminded her. "And I knew from how he had been happy to let us poke around the estate that he would want to help. You don't mind, do you?"

"Why would I mind?" her sister said archly. "What he does has nothing to do with me."

Ruby didn't look at Scarlett, but she could hear her chuckling softly.

Nate cleared his throat. "You might want to know that with Jerome's permission we exhumed the bodies in the graveyard earlier today."

"And?" Ruby asked breathily.

"You were right. The babies were likely twins. Two girls. Without DNA we can't know more yet, but the forensics expert says they were very premature and without any injuries he could see, that alone would have likely caused their death."

She leaned forward. "What about the other graves?"

"They were as the records stated. Robert Swanson and his family are buried there."

"And the lone cross?"

Nate sighed. "I was hoping you might have forgotten about that. There were several small bodies buried beneath it. Even smaller than the twins."

Ruby groaned. "All the miscarriages?"

"It's more than likely. Which means no foul play as far as forensics are concerned."

"Still, it is heartbreaking." Ruby sniffed. "So much pain and angst in one family is too tragic. Agatha had it tough after her mother died, and sadly she couldn't find it in her heart to let Meredith have it any easier."

"How could someone treat their family this way? And how could a man of the church do the things he has done?" Alex asked coldly.

He had seen the state of Meredith and how she lived. It made him so angry Ruby thought he would like to tear the minister apart for his twisted selfishness. As Alex said, Ambrose had treated Meredith doubly cruelly, by causing her to lose her babies when he gave her no option but to run away, and then wanting to lock her away himself when he had the opportunity to finally set her free. Luckily, Alex was more worried for Ruby and it was that which kept him away from the evil man.

Violet was also misty-eyed. "I just don't understand how he could look at himself in the mirror knowing that he had ruined three lives?"

"Four if you count Edgar," Ruby said sadly.

"I haven't made up my mind about him," Violet said tersely as she dabbed at her eyes. "He was so angry that day we first met him, but he was clearly docile around the minister, which allowed everything to escalate to the horrible situation Meredith found herself in. It doesn't make sense to me why he didn't stand up to the man if he loved Meredith as he says."

"Edgar was a pawn in the minister's game," Ruby spoke soothingly to her sister and included Alex. "He believed what Ambrose said, because he wanted to help his aunt who he loved more than his mother. Meredith, unfortunately, loved Ambrose. Edgar has his own issues and I believe he thought he was doing the right thing."

"I can't understand that," Alex said again. "Hiding people away because of something they did that you don't agree with or because they aren't quite right, is hateful."

"People can be cruel in all kinds of ways," Ruby reminded him gently. "If someone you trust says the words in the right way, it can seem like the best or the only answer to a problem. If we love them, maybe we say yes, when we should say no."

Alex opened his mouth then snapped it shut. His father had done that very thing. Assuring Alex that one day he would come out into the community, but not as his son—as a very good woodturner—nothing more. He had accepted his fate as an illegitimate son and decided not to make waves.

Alex understood more about Edgar than he wanted to.

He would make the best husband and father, because he knew what the alternative looked like and he would move heaven and earth not to repeat what had been done to him.

It wasn't the time to talk of weddings and babies, but Ruby made a promise to herself that as soon as this was behind them she would do exactly that. Being married to Alex was now at the top of her list and that's where she intended to keep her gentle giant.

"Eat," he said to the group, while focused solely on her.

And she knew exactly where she stood on his list.

Thanks so much for reading Deadly Desserts, the fourth book in the Cozy Cafe Mysteries series. I hope you enjoyed it!

If you did...

1 Help other people find this book by leaving a review.

2 Sign up for my new release e-mail, so you can find out about the next book as soon as it's available.

3 Come like my Facebook page.

4 Visit my website caphipps.com for all my books - buying direct costs no more!

5 Keep reading for an excerpt from Beagles Love Cupcake Crimes, Book 1 in the Beagle Diner Mysteries.

Beagles Love Cupcake Crimes

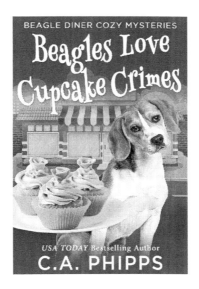

C innamon waited at the door with wet paws. Lyra followed her prints and two other drier sets of human shoe prints to the main bathroom, which was full of steam.

Dan moved back from the doorway, as did Maggie who pointed in horror at the new mirror.

Lyra frowned, then sloshed through an inch of water which had been prevented from seeping into the hallway by a mountain of towels, to where words were scrawled diagonally across the glass in condensation. Now that the hot water was turned off and the window opened, the words were fading and a couple of letters had disappeared, but it was still readable.

You don't belong here!

A shiver ran up Lyra's back. "What the heck is this about?"

"I've got no idea." Dan pointed to a sodden towel at his feet. "Whoever turned the tap on placed a towel along the door so that the water would back up. It's not too bad considering I don't know how long the tap was running, but we'll have to wait for the floor to dry out completely before the tiles go down. That will set us back a few days."

His practicality almost made her smile. Solving another mystery so soon after the last shambles was not on Lyra's plan, and it made her angry. "I don't care so much about that. The note and towel mean this was done deliberately, and I want to know why this person wants me gone. Plus, how did someone get in here without you or Cinnamon noticing?"

Dan dipped his head. "Cinnamon looked bored over by the diner, and I hadn't had my lunch, so I took her and my sandwich down by the stream. I didn't think to lock up."

He looked so miserable that Lyra forced herself to take a deep breath. "This is not your fault. We've all become lax because this isn't LA or Portland and no one seems to take security too seriously around here."

"But you're not just anyone," Maggie pointed out. "You

have fans who take liberties. They won't all disappear because you're no longer hosting a show. There is cable you know, and reruns worldwide."

"You don't seriously think a fan has followed me here?" The shiver from before reached her voice.

"Anything is possible, but that's only one scenario." Maggie attempted to reassure her. "There was a lot of drama around you buying the diner because the conglomerate wanted the whole main street knocked down and remodeled. Plus, there were those who were worried that you would bring big-city ways to town. Or maybe it's someone who wanted the diner for something else."

Lyra clenched her hands. "No matter the reason, I won't be run out of town. We need to find this troublemaker before they do something else."

"I'd like to point out that it could be a one-off," Dan suggested hopefully.

"Perhaps." Lyra liked his optimism, but she couldn't let things get out of hand the way they had in Portland and LA when she hadn't followed up hard enough after several crimes. "Meanwhile, let's make sure the house and diner are locked up if no one's there. I'll head over to the police station and tell them what happened in case they want to see the mirror or check for fingerprints around the house."

Cinnamon decided to tag along, but they were hardly down the steps when the beagle stopped. Nose twitching, she turned away from Lyra and disappeared around the side of the house. Lyra hesitated; she still had pies to fill after visiting the police, but her dog was clearly on a mission. Cinnamon sniffed around underneath the bathroom, then looked up and barked.

"What is it, girl?"

The beagle sat and lifted her right paw, still looking up.

There was a slight slope leading down to the stream, and a small tree sat close to the window. From one of the branches hung a hat. Lyra stretched up on her tippy toes and yanked it free.

Fairview Forever was emblazoned on the rim. "I've seen these around, Cin. Do you think the person who broke in and left the taps on dropped this?"

The beagle wagged her tail and looked up again as Dan poked his head out the open window.

"I thought I heard you talking." He smirked.

"Look what Cinnamon found on that shrub." Lyra waved the hat at him. "Did you leave the bathroom window open when you were out?"

He blinked. "Now that you mention it, I thought I had, but it was closed when I got back."

"Hmmm. That implies that the person either went in or came out the window," Lyra mused. "Maybe both. Perhaps while they were trying to close the window, they lost the hat."

Maggie joined Dan at the window and leaned on the sash. "That makes sense because there were no wet footprints inside the house other than ours. They had to have left this way unless they didn't wait for the sink to overflow."

"The hot water had to run a while to fog the mirror, and the window would need to be closed." Lyra paced around the tree. "Can you see there are a couple of broken branches at the top? They have to be strong enough to hold their weight, so it can't be a small person."

"Although, those branches aren't terribly thick," Maggie noted.

"You reached the hat," Dan pointed out. "Which means the person must be shorter than you."

"True, but maybe they heard you arrive, were in a hurry to get away, and simply didn't have time to collect the hat."

Rob McKenna poked his head around the corner. "Seems like a funny place to have a party."

"No party; it's more of a brainstorm," Lyra explained. "Somebody broke into the house and turned a tap on. The bathroom was flooded, but Dan caught it in time before it spread through the rest of the house."

"Well done, lad. That could have been nasty after all your hard work. Any ideas on the culprit?"

"None, but they left this hat hanging on a shrub." Lyra held it out to him.

"It looks pretty worn, but I'm sorry to say that most residents have one of them, including me." Rob shrugged. "Seems to me that it could have been left by anyone at any time."

"Really?" Lyra twisted the hat in her hands. "That's a shame. I thought it was a great clue."

"Sorry to burst your bubble. The town committee got a bunch of them made up when we had a fishing competition a while ago. It was back when we were being proactive about getting tourists and some new residents."

"You mean that not only people from Fairview might have one of these caps?"

"Unfortunately, that's likely true."

"Darn it." Lyra sighed. "I thought we might be onto something."

"Well, if anyone says they lost their cap, I'll let you know," Rob said, deadpan.

He loved to tease, and this wasn't such a big deal, but what if it heralded the beginning of something worse? While she wasn't naturally pessimistic, recent history had slightly scarred her optimism about such things. "I guess the likelihood of that happening is remote. Since it's not life-or-death, we haven't rung the police, but I'm going to the station to report this."

"I'll come with you," he offered. "Sheriff Walker can be hard to talk to."

Lyra didn't doubt that. The times he came in for coffee or a bite he had stared far too much for her liking. He was good-looking with short brown hair which made his cool gray eyes even more startling. And piercing. She got the impression he didn't know what to make of her and she felt the same about him.

"In that case, I'll be glad of the company." She looked up to find Dan and Maggie gazing at each other. "Could you two clean up the water, but leave the mirror and keep Cinnamon here?"

It could have been the sun warming their faces, but both were pink-cheeked.

"Leave it to us," Dan called, then moved back into the room.

The station wasn't far. They crossed the street at the end of Lyra's drive, went up the road, and passed a couple of houses. When they got to the corner, they crossed again. The station was five doors down, and Rob explained that it was usually manned by three police officers. Also, the sheriff had towns to the east and west that he oversaw, so he wasn't always there.

The few times she'd seen him in the street, or when he'd stopped by for coffee, he'd given her a penetrating look that was both embarrassing and annoying. Naturally he would have heard rumors about her troubled past and quite possibly investigated them. Which should have exonerated her from anything that he could dig up. Whatever his reason for being less than friendly, she didn't like it one bit.

"I hope this isn't our designated walk for today. Even if you have provided a little more drama than usual," Rob teased.

"You can't get out of it that easily. Besides, Cinnamon won't be happy that we've left her behind."

He nodded. "She does like her freedom."

Rob opened the door for Lyra, and inside they found the desk clerk reading a romance novel. Her badge read Officer Moore, and when she noticed them, she quickly stuffed the book under the counter.

"Ms. St. Claire, what can I do for you?" she gushed.

Lyra had seen this kind of reaction so many times it hardly affected her, and she quickly explained the situation. When she finished, the clerk blinked several times before responding.

"Goodness, that's a tricky one. With almost everyone owning a hat like that, I don't know how we can say who did this."

Lyra breathed deeply. "Officer Moore, I appreciate that right now we can't pin it on anyone, and the writing on the mirror will be gone," Belatedly, it occurred to her that she should have taken a photo, "but is there a chance that someone could come take a look at the crime scene?"

The officer shot a longing glance at where she'd stowed the book. "I guess it couldn't hurt. Let me speak to the sheriff."

Lyra sighed as the woman disappeared out the back and took a seat on a hard wooden bench. "We might be here a while."

"It could be worse." Rob dropped the words enigmatically and sat beside her.

They waited for ten minutes, scanning all the brochures on display, until the sheriff appeared. Tall and roughly

Dan's build, his hair was pressed down on top as if he'd recently worn a hat. He ran those cool gray eyes over Lyra, then grimaced at Rob.

"Officer Moore told me about your problem, Ms. St. Claire. It seems a little far-fetched that someone would break in to cause a flood. Are you sure that your handyman didn't leave the tap on?"

His dismissive attitude rankled, and it was an effort to be polite. "Thank you for seeing us. I understand that it's not much to go on, but if Dan had done that, he would have told me so. And why would he leave a note on the mirror telling me I didn't belong here when he lives in my house? Also, I know he doesn't have a cap like this." Lyra handed it to him.

The sheriff turned it over a couple of times in an unconcerned manner. "While it's commendable that you trust your handyman, it just doesn't seem like something that would happen around here. Maybe Dan would prefer to get back to the big city sooner than you thought. Now that the major building has been completed, an ex-army man probably has a few more abilities other than doing odd jobs. As for the cap, I'm sure Rob told you they're a dime a dozen and could have been left there by anyone before you showed up—or after."

Lyra stiffened at the mention of Dan wanting more than working for her. It sounded as though the sheriff had been doing some checks on the town's newest inhabitants and made a few judgements. "I can assure you that Dan is free to leave whenever he chooses and has no need to make up ridiculous scenarios to do so. Finding out why that cap was stuck in a tree outside my bathroom would be a better question?"

He shrugged. "It gets windy around town. I dare say it blew there."

"Since I've been in Fairview, it hasn't been windy at all."

Sheriff Walker narrowed his eyes as if she'd called him a liar. "Lucky for you. Now, if you're done, I need to get back to solving real crimes for our residents."

Irritated by his dismissal, Lyra noted he kept the cap.

"Thanks for dropping by. I do love your food, and your show was amazing," Officer Moore gushed. "It's such a shame that you lost it."

Lyra simply nodded as they left. People couldn't appreciate that she was happy to give up her fame for a diner in Fairview. "How about that? He wasn't the slightest bit interested," she told Rob when they got outside the door.

"I confess that I was curious if you'd have more sway with Walker than me. Since he was giving me the side-eye, I decided to keep my mouth shut, but it seems he treats most people with the same disdain."

"I guess a flood isn't high on a priority list. We were lucky that Dan found it when he did."

"Don't you fret. As much as it doesn't seem like it, the sheriff doesn't like drama in his towns, so he won't sit by and do nothing, and I'll keep an eye on the house."

The sheriff's style of working was certainly interesting, but she wasn't satisfied with the outcome. "Even if we all took turns, it's not possible to watch it all day. We have businesses to run, and Dan and Maggie are busy too."

"I take on less work these days, so I have time to wander by. I'll make it known around town that there was a break-in. If someone's worried about getting caught, they won't like that, and the rest of us will be more vigilant."

"Thanks for the help, but last thing I want is for you to put yourself in danger."

"A person who turns on a tap isn't likely bent on physically hurting another." Rob scratched the top of his head. "In my opinion, your tap-turner is a coward."

"I hope you're right. Please be careful, and call Dan if you see anything. Now, I better get my pies done, the pastry will be ruined and I'll have to start over."

About to part company at the corner, Rob raised an eyebrow. "We can't have that. Perhaps I better check one to make sure they're okay before you try to sell any."

Lyra groaned. "Another tester—just what I need. Come by in an hour, and they'll be ready."

"No need to twist my arm." He waved and swaggered toward his garage, several doors down the street from their houses.

One of the unforeseen pleasures of coming home to Fairview was her next-door neighbor always made her laugh.

Need to know what happens next? Get your copy of Book 1 in the Beagle Diner Cozy Mystery Series, Beagles Love Cupcake Crimes now!

Recipes

These recipes are ones I use all the time and have come down the generations from my mum, grandmother, and some I have adapted from other recipes. Also, I now have my husband's grandmother's recipe book. Exciting! I'll be bringing some of them to life very soon.

Just a wee reminder, that I am a New Zealander. Occasionally I may have missed converting into ounces and pounds for my American readers.

My apologies for that, and please let me know—if you do try them—how they turn out.

Cheryl x

Pumpkin Pie

Ingredients

  2 cups mashed pumpkin (cooled)

  1 can of sweetened condensed milk

  2 eggs

  1 tsp ground cinnamon

  1/2 tsp ground ginger

  1/2 tsp ground nutmeg

  1/2 tsp salt

  1 sheet of sweet short pastry

Instructions

  1 Preheat oven to 425F / 220 C

  2 Cut pastry sheet to fit a 9 inch pie tin.

  3 Fill pie crust with beans or rice on top of baking paper and bake for 12 - 15 minutes or until pastry is beginning to brown.

  4 Whisk all ingredients until smooth and pour into cooled pastry.

  5 Bake for 10 minutes then reduce heat to 360F/ 180C and bake until pastry is golden brown.

6 Leave to cool and set.

7 Slice and serve with whipped cream or yoghurt.

Also by C. A. Phipps

Midlife Potions - Paranormal Cozy Mysteries

Witchy Awakening

Witchy Hot Spells

Witchy Flash Back

Witchy Bad Blood - preorder now!

The Cozy Café Mysteries

Sweet Saboteur

Candy Corruption

Mocha Mayhem

Berry Betrayal

Deadly Desserts

The Maple Lane Cozy Mysteries

Sugar and Sliced - Maple Lane Prequel

Apple Pie and Arsenic

Bagels and Blackmail

Cookies and Chaos

Doughnuts and Disaster

Eclairs and Extortion

Fudge and Frenemies

Gingerbread and Gunshots

Honey Cake and Homicide - coming soon!

Beagle Diner Cozy Mysteries

Beagles Love Cupcake Crimes

Beagles Love Steak Secrets

Beagles Love Muffin But Murder

Beagles Love Layer Cake Lies - preorder now!

Please note: Most are also available in paperback and some in audio.

Remember to join Cheryl's Cozy Mystery newsletter.

There's a free recipe book waiting for you. ;-)

Cheryl also writes romance as Cheryl Phipps.

About the author

'Life is a mystery. Let's follow the clues together.'

C. A. Phipps is a USA Today best-selling author from beautiful New Zealand. Cheryl lives in a quiet suburb with her wonderful husband, whom she married the moment she left school (yes, they were high school sweethearts). With three married children and seven grandchildren to keep her busy when she's not writing, there is just enough space for a crazy mixed breed dog who stole her heart! She loves family times, baking, rambling walks, and her quest for the perfect latte.

Check out her website http://caphipps.com

facebook.com/authorcaphipps

x.com/CherylAPhipps

instagram.com/caphippsauthor

Printed in Great Britain
by Amazon

31323078R00126